Dearest Alicia, with love & best wishes for your 2nd birthday.

Gillian & Sarah Oppler.

EDMVND DVLAC'S
FAIRY-BOOK

THE BURIED MOON

"In her frantic struggles the hood of her cloak fell
back from her dazzling golden hair, and immediately the
whole place was flooded with light."

Page 15

EDMVND DVLAC'S FAIRY-BOOK

FAIRY TALES OF THE ALLIED NATIONS

PORTLAND HOVSE
NEW YORK

This 1988 edition is published by Portland House, a division of
dilithium Press, Ltd., distributed by Crown Publishers, Inc.,
225 Park Avenue South, New York, New York 10003.

Printed and bound in the United States of America

Library of Congress Cataloging-in-Publication Data

Edmund Dulac's fairy-book.

   Summary: A reprinting of a collection of folk and fairy tales from
Belgium, France, England, Japan, Italy, and Serbia.
   1. Fairy tales. 2. Tales. [1. Fairy tales. 2. Folklore] I. Dulac,
Edmund, 1882-1953, ill.
PZ8.E234   1988   398.2'1   88-25809
ISBN 0-517-67583-8

h g f e d c b a

CONTENTS

CONTENTS

CONTENTS

ILLUSTRATIONS IN COLOR

ILLUSTRATIONS IN COLOR

ILLUSTRATIONS IN COLOR

FOREWORD

WHEN, in 1915, the Leicester Galleries in England proposed to Edmund Dulac that he illustrate a book of Russian fairy tales, he eagerly took on the assignment. But it was soon evident to this multitalented man that a book with a more varied contents would have greater appeal and therefore greater sales. It was during the time of World War I, and the notion of creating a fairy tale book with stories from all of the Allied nations seemed not only patriotic but also commercially promising. The project thus involved the inclusion of fairy stories from Belgium, France, England, Japan, Italy, and Serbia. It seems likely that Dulac, as illustrator and orchestrator of the book, chose all of the tales to be used, and the Leicester Galleries, as commissioner of the book, probably helped in the selection. Together, they assimilated a collection of predominantly unfamiliar stories, each of which is so packed with surprises, unusual twists, absurd premises, and totally unpredictable consequences that one must shake one's head in disbelief and delight with the turning of almost every page.

Edmund Dulac's Fairy-Book was created during the Golden Age of illustrated children's books, a time when it was technically and financially possible to mass-produce beautifully bound books with tipped-in color illustrations. Now, with this re-creation of the original book, we are able to experience the timeless appeal that really good fairy tales hold for children and the child in grownups alike.

Each tale in this volume is a treasure in itself. To reveal too much of the plots would spoil the pleasure that each reader has in store; but a little preview seems prudent (and, really, it is all that is possible to give, so complex are so many of the tales!).

FOREWORD

The tales are unusually creative, as any really good literature must be. Masterful science fiction, mystery, and the lure of the unknown are evident in stories such as "The Queen of the Many-Coloured Bedchamber," from Ireland:

> It was some two hours before dawn when they descried, in the distance, the lighted tower of the witch, upon an island. A dull, red flame shot out from it, and, as it turned for ever on itself, this flame lighted the sea around like a revolving wheel, clear and red against the surrounding blackness.

and in the Russian classic, "The Fire Bird":

> Eager to find out where this light came from, and seeing his way more clearly now, he hastened on, and soon arrived at the mouth of a large cave, which, inside, was as bright as day. He ventured farther forward and peered around a buttress of rock; and there, in the centre of the cave, a strange sight met his eyes. A gigantic bird was standing there, getting ready to fly through the farther opening overlooking the valley. It was stretching its neck and flapping its wings; and, from every feather of these, flashed rays and sparkles of light, illuminating the whole place.

Most fairy tales have at least some wishes in them if they are worth their salt, but seldom are wishes so extraordinary as we find in the English fairy tale, "The Friar and the Boy":

> Jack pondered a long time, and at last he chuckled and clapped his hands with glee. When the old man asked him what tickled him so, he could not reply at once, as he was so busy enjoying some joke beforehand. At last, when he was able to speak, he said, 'Father, it has just crossed my mind that my stepmother is always looking at me sourly and always scolding me. I wish that when she does this she will laugh, and go on laughing till I give her the word to stop. Can you grant that wish, father?'

For sheer complicated revelations, nothing can beat the passage in "Bashtchelik (or Real Steel)," the Serbian tale, where Bashtchelik reveals the source of his strength:

> Far away in a high tableland in the interior of this country there is a mountain reaching up to the sky, and rooted far down into the earth. In a spot of that mountain—in a den where a serpent lies asleep—there is

xiv

a fox, and in its heart there hides a bird. That bird is the storehouse of my strength.

We are all used to fairy tales where there is a test to locate the rightful match for the prince or princess. But the prize for creative romance goes to the Russian, "Ivan and the Chestnut Horse":

> The King's daughter, Princess Helena the Fair, has caused to be built for herself a shrine having twelve pillars and twelve rows of beams. And she sits there upon a high throne till the time when the bridegroom of her choice rides by. And this is how she shall know him: with one leap of his steed he reaches the height of the tower, and, in passing, his lips press those of the Princess as she bends from her throne.

The range of stories and styles more than meets the reader's expectations. The book opens with the charming Russian "Snegorotchka," a familiar Pinocchio-like tale of a created child. "The Buried Moon" is reminiscent of Thomas Hardy in its descriptions of English bogs, but reminiscent of no other story in the simple tale it tells. Adventure and romance are ingredients of most of the stories, but the best romances are the Italian "The Serpent Prince," the French "The Blue Bird," and the French "The Green Serpent." The Japanese "Urashima Taro" is a bittersweet ocean romance, and the Irish "The Queen of the Many-Coloured Bedchamber" has one of the wickedest witches in memory upsetting things until the final moments. For comedy, "The Friar and the Boy" is sheer delight; and for adventure, the Belgian "The Seven Conquerors of the Queen of the Mississippi" and "Bashtchelik," the Serbian tale, are top-notch. "The Hind of the Wood," more familiar than most in this volume, has a few minor differences from other versions; it always holds the interest of children and adults alike with its wicked spell, waiting to be broken. But the gentle white hind is such an endearing victim that our journey through the tale is buffered and caressed by the hind's presence. The book ends with much the same charming simplicity with which it began, offering "The Story of the Bird Feng" with its perfect oriental delicacy and ephemeral quality.

FOREWORD

The variety of the stories is matched only by the variety of their illustrator's gifts. In addition to creating beautiful pictures for books, Edmund Dulac designed postage stamps (including one for the coronation of Queen Elizabeth II), scenery and costumes for the stage, furniture, was both a composer and an author, and a friend of such diverse people as Sir Thomas Beecham and William Butler Yeats. It is therefore not surprising to find that he has assembled a collection of stories such as this. For he had a remarkable sensitivity and imagination which is evident not only in his illustrations for this book, but also in his ability to catch the unusual among the thousands of fairy tales at his disposal.

We, as readers, can be grateful for Dulac's care and talent and for the period which enabled him to grow and to produce for us. As with any great work of art, the artist may have a specific goal in mind (such as a collection of fairy tales from the Allied nations), and if it is done superbly, it will outlast its origins and become a classic for all time. Certainly *Edmund Dulac's Fairy-Book* has accomplished this. It is a tribute to Dulac, to the Golden Age of children's literature, and to the development of and appreciation for imagination in us all.

Durham, North Carolina   PATRICIA B. PERKINS
1988

ABOUT EDMUND DULAC AND HIS ART

EDMUND DULAC (1882–1953) was born in Toulouse, France. During his adolescence, his developing artistic sense was deeply influenced by Japanese woodcuts imported by his uncle. In 1904, frustrated by the academic style of the art taught in the Paris schools, and seeking a more hospitable environment for his talents, Dulac left France for England. He began his career as a book illustrator in London.

From the beginning Dulac had an affinity for Eastern art. One can see this influence in the oriental patterning of the palanquin borne by the four elephants in "The Serpent Prince," giving subtle texture as well as ornament. The positioning of the scene high on the page in "The Buried Moon," away from the foreground, is very Japanese; so are the mask-like faces of the characters in "The Blue Bird." All have the richness of color and detail associated with Persian miniatures.

Dulac was a meticulous craftsman. His book illustrations are careful, planned compositions much like jeweled miniatures. In the beginning of his career, he used only pencil and watercolor as his medium for book illustration; later he added crayon for additional weight and texture.

Over and over again Dulac drew the face of his ideal woman into his illustrations, beginning at first with his (second) wife Elsa, and soon changing to the neo-classical face of Helen Beauclerk, with whom he lived out the rest of his life after his marriage ended. Helen's distinctive dark hair, high cheekbones, and long forehead may be seen in "The Story of Urashima Taro," "The Story of the Bird Feng," and many others.

xvii

ABOUT EDMUND DULAC

Dulac used light in much the same way as color. His subjects are illuminated by radiance from an invisible source or by visible prisms such as stars gleaming jewel-like in the sky. The color plates in the *Fairy-Book* are remarkable not only for their art, but for their total absorption with the stories; they literally take you into the story world with an intensity that transcends ordinary visual imagination. The tiny girl in "Snegorotchka" is all white against white snow, chilling and warming in the same glance; the palace of the Dragon King in "Bashtchelik" rests high in the mountains—glittering, luxurious domes surrounded by hissing snakes of incredible size. The "Fire Bird" is orange, yellow, flame red, with green peacock eyes on its wings, and it flies in star-lit cobalt skies above the nocturnal garden where a Princess sleeps.

To discover the intricate pleasures of Dulac's illustrations is to open a fairy-garden of visual delight. His remarkable watercolors enrich the imagination, causing the stories to catch fire and burn their images into our minds, until the shadows fly high in the night skies of our dreams, much like his marvelous Fire Bird.

LOIS HILL

New York
1988

xviii

EDITORIAL NOTE

THE modern reader may be surprised to discover certain old-fashioned and British styles of punctuation and spelling, but these have been retained in order to convey the flavor of the original edition.

SNEGOROTCHKA

A RUSSIAN FAIRY TALE

THE old wife sang merrily as she sat in the inglenook*stirring the soup, for she had never felt so sad. Many, many years had come and gone, leaving the weight of their winters on her shoulders and the touch of snow on her hair without ever bringing her a little child. This made her and her dear old husband very sad, for there were many children outside, playing in the snow. It seemed hard that not even one among them was their very own. But alas! there was no hope for such a blessing now. Never would they see a little fur cap hanging on the corner of the mantelpiece, nor two little shoes drying by the fire.

The old husband brought in a bundle of wood and set it down. Then, as he heard the children laughing and clapping their hands outside, he looked out at the window. There they were, dancing with glee round a snow man they had made. He smiled as he saw that it was evidently meant to look like the Mayor of the village, it was so fat and pompous.

'Look, Marusha!' he cried to the old wife. 'Come and see the snow man they've made.'

As they stood together at the window, they laughed to see what fun the children got out of it. Suddenly the old man turned to her with a bright idea.

'Let's go out and see if *we* can't make a little snow man.'

But Marusha laughed at him. 'What would the neighbours say? They would poke fun at us; it'd be the joke of the village. Besides, we're too old to play like children.'

'But only a little one, Marusha; only a teeny-weeny little snow man,—and I'll manage it that nobody sees us.'

9

*Inglenook, chimney corner

SNEGOROTCHKA

'Well, well,' she said, laughing; 'have your own way, as you always did, Youshko.'

With this she took the pot from the fire, put on her bonnet, and they went out together. As they passed the children, they stopped to play with them a while, for they now felt almost like children themselves. Then they trudged on through the snow till they came to a clump of trees, and, behind this, where the snow was nice and white, and nobody could see them, they set to work to make their little man.

The old husband insisted that it must be very small, and the old wife agreed that it should be almost as small as a new-born babe. Kneeling down in the snow, they fashioned the little body in next to no time. Now there remained only the head to finish. Two fat handfuls of snow for the cheeks and face, and a big one on top for the head. Then they put on a wee dab for the nose and poked two holes, one on each side, for the eyes.

It was soon done, and they were already standing back looking at it, and laughing and clapping their hands like children. Then suddenly they stopped. What had happened? A very strange thing indeed! Out of the two holes they saw looking at them two wistful blue eyes. Then the face of the little snow man was no longer white. The cheeks became rounded and smooth and radiant, and two rosy lips began to smile up at them. A breath of wind brushed the snow from the head, and it all fell down round the shoulders in flaxen ringlets escaping from a white fur cap. At the same time some snow, loosened from the little body, fell down and took the shape of a pretty white garment. Then, suddenly, before they could open and shut their mouths, their snow mannikin was gone, and in his place stood the daintiest, prettiest little maiden they had ever seen.

They gave each other a look out of the corners of their eyes, and scratched their heads in wonderment. But it was as true as true. There stood the little girl, all pink and white before them. She was really alive, for she ran to them; and, when they stooped down to lift her up, she put one arm round the old wife's neck and the other round the old man's, and gave them each a hug and a kiss.

They laughed and cried for joy; then, suddenly remembering how real some dreams can seem, they pinched each other in turn. Still they were not sure, for the pinches might have been a part of the dream. So, in fear lest they might wake and spoil the whole thing, they wrapped the little girl up quickly and hastened back home.

On the way they met the children, still playing round their snow man; and the snowballs with which they pelted them in the back were very real; but there again, the snowballs might have belonged to the dream. But when they were inside the house, and saw the inglenook, with the soup in the pot by the fire and the bundle of wood near by, and everything just as they had left it, they looked at each other with tears in their eyes and no longer feared that it was all a dream. In another minute there was a little white fur cap hanging on the corner of the mantelpiece and two little shoes drying by the fire, while the old wife took the little girl on her lap and crooned a lullaby over her.

The old man put his hand on his wife's shoulder and she looked up.

'Marusha!'

'Youshko!'

'At last we have a little girl! We made her out of the snow, so we will call her Snegorotchka.'

The old wife nodded her head, and then they kissed each other. When they had all had supper, they went to bed, the old husband and wife feeling sure that they would wake early in the morning to find the child still with them. And they were not disappointed. There she was, sitting up between them, prattling and laughing. But she had grown bigger, and her hair was now twice as long as at first. When she called them 'Little Father' and 'Little Mother' they were so delighted that they felt like dancing as nimbly as they had in their young days. But, instead of dancing, they just kissed each other, and wept for joy.

That day they held a big feast. The old wife was busy all the morning cooking all kinds of dainties, while the old man went round the village and collected the fiddlers. All the boys and girls of the village were invited, and they ate and sang and danced and had a merry time till daybreak. As they went home, the girls all talked at once about how much they had enjoyed themselves, but the boys were very silent;—they were thinking of the beautiful Snegorotchka with the blue eyes and the golden hair.

Every day after that Snegorotchka played with the other children, and taught them how to make castles and palaces of snow, with marble halls and thrones and beautiful fountains. The snow seemed to let her do whatever she liked with it, and to build itself up under her tiny fingers as if it knew exactly what shape it was to take. They were all greatly delighted with the wonderful things she made ; but when she showed them how to dance as the snow-flakes do, first in a brisk whirl, and then softly and lightly, they could think of nothing else but Snegorotchka. She was the little fairy queen of the children, the delight of the older people, and the very breath of life to old Marusha and Youshko.

And now the winter months moved on. With slow and steady stride they went from mountain top to mountain top, around the circle of the sky-line. The earth began to clothe itself in green. The great trees, holding out their naked arms like huge babies waiting to be dressed, were getting greener and greener, and last year's birds sat in their branches singing this year's songs. The early flowers shed their perfume on the breeze, and now and then a waft of warm air, straying from its summer haunts, caressed the cheek and breathed a glowing promise in the ear. The forests and the fields were stirring. A beautiful spirit brooded over the face of nature ;—spring was trembling on the leash and tugging to be free.

One afternoon Marusha was sitting in the inglenook stirring

the soup and singing a mournful song, because she had never felt so full of joy. The old man Youshko had just brought in a bundle of wood and laid it on the hearth. It seemed just the same as on that winter's afternoon when they saw the children dancing round their snow man; but what made all the difference was Snegorotchka, the apple of their eye, who now sat by the window, gazing out at the green grass and the budding trees.

Youshko had been looking at her; he had noticed that her face was pale and her eyes a shade less blue than usual. He grew anxious about her.

'Are you not feeling well, Snegorotchka?' he asked.

'No, Little Father,' she replied sadly. 'I miss the white snow,—oh! so much; the green grass is not half as beautiful. I wish the snow would come again.'

'Oh! yes; the snow will come again,' replied the old man. 'But don't you like the leaves on the trees and the blossoms and the flowers, my darling?'

'They are not so beautiful as the pure, white snow.' And Snegorotchka shuddered.

The next day she looked so pale and sad that they were alarmed, and glanced at one another anxiously.

'What ails the child?' said Marusha.

Youshko shook his head and looked from Snegorotchka to the fire, and then back again.

'My child,' he said at last, 'why don't you go out and play with the others? They are all enjoying themselves among the flowers in the forest; but I've noticed you never play with them now. Why is it, my darling?'

'I don't know, Little Father, but my heart seems to turn to water when the soft warm wind brings the scent of the blossoms.'

'But we will come with you, my child,' said the old man. 'I will put my arm about you and shield you from the wind. Come, we will show you all the pretty flowers in the grass, and tell you their names, and you will just love them,—all of them.'

SNEGOROTCHKA

So Marusha took the pot off the fire and then they all went out together, Youshko with his arm round Snegorotchka to shield her from the wind. But they had not gone far when the warm perfume of the flowers was wafted to them on the breeze, and the child trembled like a leaf. They both comforted her and kissed her, and then they went on towards the spot where the flowers grew thickly in the grass. But, as they passed a clump of big trees, a bright ray of sunlight struck through like a dart and Snegorotchka put her hand over her eyes and gave a cry of pain.

They stood still and looked at her. For a moment, as she drooped upon the old man's arm, her eyes met theirs; and on her upturned face were swiftly running tears which sparkled in the sunlight as they fell. Then, as they watched her, she grew smaller and smaller, until, at last, all that was left of Snegorotchka was a little patch of dew shining on the grass. One tear-drop had fallen into the cup of a flower. Youshko gathered that flower—very gently —and handed it to Marusha without a word.

They both understood now. Their darling was just a little girl made of snow, and she had melted away in the warmth of the sunlight.

THE BURIED MOON

AN ENGLISH FAIRY TALE

In my old Granny's days, long, long—oh, so long ago, Carland was just a collection of bogs. Pools of black water lay in the hollows, and little green rivulets scurried away here and there like long lizards trying to escape from their tails, while every tuft that you trod upon would squirt up at you like anything. Oh! it *was* a nice place to be in on a dark night, I give you my word.

Now, I've heard my Granny say that a long time before her day the Moon got trapped and buried in the bog. I'll tell you the tale as she used to tell it to me.

On some nights the beautiful Moon rose up in the sky and shone brighter and brighter, and the people blessed her because by her wonderful light they could find their way home at night through the treacherous bogs. But on other nights she did not come, and then it was so dark that the traveller could not find his way; and, besides, the Evil Things that feared the light—toads and creepy, crawly things, to say nothing of Bogles*and Little Bad People— came out in the darkness to do all the harm they could, for they hated the people and were always trying to lead them astray. Many a poor man going home in the dark had been enticed by these malevolent things into quicksands and mud pools. When the Moon was away and the night was black, these vile creatures had their will.

When the Moon learned about this, she was very grieved, for she is a sweet, kind body, who spends nights without sleep, so as to show a light for people going home. She was troubled about it all, and said to herself, ' I'll just go down and see how matters stand.'

15

Bogles, goblins

So, when the dark end of the month came round, she stepped down out of the sky, wrapped from head to foot in her black travelling cloak with the hood drawn over her bright golden hair. For a moment she stood at the edge of the marshes, looking this way and that. Everywhere, as far as she could see, was the dismal bog, with pools of black water, and gnarled, fantastic-looking snags sticking up here and there amid the dank growth of weeds and grasses. There was no light save the feeble glimmer of the stars reflected in the gloomy pools ; but, upon the grass where she stood, a bright ring of moonlight shone from her feet beneath her cloak.

She saw this and drew her garments closer about her. It was cold, and she was trembling. She feared that vast expanse of bog and its evil creatures, but she was determined to face the matter out and see exactly how the thing stood.

Guided by the light that streamed from her feet, she advanced into the bog. As the summer wind stirs one tussock*after another, so she stepped onward between the slimy ponds and deadly quag-mires. Now she reached a jet-black pool, and all too late she saw the stars shining in its depths. Her foot tripped and all she could do was to snatch at an overhanging branch of a snag as she fell forward. To this she clung, but, fast as she gripped it, faster still some tendrils from the bough whipped round her wrists like manacles and held her there a prisoner. She struggled and wrenched and tugged with all her might and main, but the tendrils only tightened and cut into her wrists like steel bands.

As she stood there shivering in the dark and wondering how to free herself, she heard far away in the bog a voice calling through the night. It was a wailing cry, dying away in despair. She listened and listened, and the repeated cry came nearer ; then she heard footsteps—halting, stumbling and slipping. At last, by the dim light of the stars, she saw a haggard, despairing face with fearful eyes ; and then she knew it was a poor man who had lost his way and was floundering on to his death. Now he caught sight of a gleam of light from the captive Moon, and made his uncertain way

16

Tussock, tuft of grass

towards it, thinking it meant help. As he came nearer and nearer the pool, the Moon saw that her light was luring him to his death, and she felt so very sorry for him, and so angry with herself that she struggled fiercely at the cords that held her. It was all in vain, but, in her frantic struggles, the hood of her cloak fell back from her dazzling golden hair, and immediately the whole place was flooded with light, which fell on muddy pools and quicks and quags, glinting on the twisted roots and making the whole place as clear as day.

How glad the wayfarer was to see the light! How pleased he was to see all the Evil Things of the dark scurrying back into their holes! He could now find his way, and he made for the edge of the treacherous marsh with such haste that he had not time to wonder at the strange thing that had happened. He did not know that the blessed light that showed him his path to safety shone from the radiant hair of the Moon, bound fast to a snag and half buried in the bog. And the Moon herself was so glad he was safe, that she forgot her own danger and need. But, as she watched him making good his escape from the terrible dangers of the marshes, she was overcome by a great longing to follow him. This made her tug and strain again like a demented creature, until she sank exhausted, but not free, in the mud at the foot of the snag. As she did so, her head fell forward on her breast, and the hood of her cloak again covered her shining hair.

At that moment, just as suddenly as the light had shone out before, the darkness came down with a swish, and all the vile things that loved it came out of their hiding-places with a kind of whispering screech which grew louder and louder as they swarmed abroad on the marshes. Now they gathered round the poor Moon, snarling and scratching at her and screaming hateful mockeries at her. At last they had her in their power—their old foe whose light they could not endure; the Bright One whose smile of light sent them scurrying away into their crevices and defeated their fell designs.

'Hell roast thee!' cried an ugly old witch-thing; 'thou 'rt the meddlesome body that spoils all our brews.'

'Out on thee!' shrieked the bogle-bodies; 'if 'twere not for thee we 'd have the marsh to ourselves.'

And there was a great clamour—as out-of-tune as out-of-tune could be. All the things of darkness raised their harsh and cracked voices against the Bright One of the sky. 'Ha, ha!' and 'Ho, ho!' and 'He, he!' mingled with chuckles of fiendish glee, until it seemed as if the very trickles and gurgles of the bog were joining in the orgy of hate.

'Burn her with corpse-lights!' yelled the witch.

'Ha, ha! He, he!' came the chorus of evil creatures.

'Truss her up and stifle her!' screamed the creeping things. 'Spin webs round her!' And the spiders of the night swarmed all over her.

'Sting her to death!' said the Scorpion King at the head of his brood.

'Ho, ho! He, he!' And, as each vile thing had something to say about it, a horrible, screeching dispute arose, while the captive Moon crouched shuddering at the foot of the snag and gave herself up as lost.

The dim grey light of the early dawn found them still hissing and clawing and screeching at one another as to the best way to dispose of the captive. Then, when the first rosy ray shot up from the Sun, they grew afraid. Some scuttled away, but those who remained hastened to do something—anything that would smother the light of the Moon. The only thing they could think of now was to bury her in the mud,—bury her deep. They were all agreed on this as the quickest way.

So they clutched her with skinny fingers and pushed her down into the black mud beneath the water at the foot of the snag. When they had all stamped upon her, the bogle-bodies ran quickly and fetched a big black stone which they hurled on top of her to keep her down. Then the old witch called two will-o'-the-wisps from the darkest part of the marshes, and, when they came dancing and glancing above the pools and quicks,* she bade them keep watch by the grave of the Moon, and, if she tried to get out, to sound an alarm.

Then the horrid things crept away from the morning light, chuckling to themselves over the funeral of the Moon, and only wishing they could bury the Sun in the same way; but that was a little too much to hope for, and besides, all respectable Horrors of the Bog ought to be asleep in bed during the Sun's journey across the sky.

The poor Moon was now buried deep in the black mud, with a heavy stone on top of her. Surely she could never again thwart their plans of evil, hatched and nurtured in the foul darkness of the quags. She was buried deep; they had left no sign; who would know where to look for her?

Day after day passed by until the time of the New Moon was eagerly looked for by the good folk who dwelt around the marshes, for they knew they had no friend like the Moon, whose light enabled them to find the pathways through the bog-land, and drove away all the vile things into their dark holes and corners. So they put lucky pennies in their pouches and straws in their hats, and searched for the crescent Moon in the sky. But evening twilight brought no Moon, which was not strange, for she was buried deep in the bog.

The nights were pitch dark, and the Horrors held frolic in the marshes and swarmed abroad in ever-increasing numbers, so that no traveller was safe. The poor people were so frightened and dumbfounded at being forsaken by the friendly Moon, that some of them went to the old Wise Woman of the Mill and besought her to find out what was the matter.

The Wise Woman gazed long into her magic mirror, and then made a brew of herbs, into which she looked just as long, muttering words that nobody but herself could understand.

'It's very strange,' she said at last; 'but there's nought to say

*Quicks, brush or thickets

what has become of her. I'll look again later on; meantime if ye do learn anything, let me know.'

So they went away more mystified than ever, and, as the following nights brought no Moon, they could do nothing but stand about in groups in the streets discussing the strange thing. The disappearance of the Moon was the one topic. By the fireside, at the work-bench, in the inn and all about, their tongues went nineteen to the dozen; and no wonder, for who had ever heard of the Moon being lost, stolen or strayed?

But it chanced one day that a man from the other side of the marshes was sitting in the inn, smoking his pipe and listening to the talk of the other inmates, when all of a sudden he sat bolt upright, slapped his thigh and cried out, 'I' fegs! Now I mind where that there Moon be!'

Then he told them how one night he had got lost in the marshes and was frightened to death; how he went blundering on in the dark with all the Evil Things after him, and, at last, how a great bright light burst out of a pool and showed him the way to go.

When they heard this they all took the shortest cut to the Wise Woman, and told her the man's story. After a long look in the mirror and the pot, she wagged her head slowly and said, 'It's all dark, children. You see, being as there's no Moon to conjure by, I can't tell ye where she's gone or what's made off with her—which same I could tell ye fine if she was in her right place. But mebbe, if ye do what I'm going to tell ye, then ye may hap on her yourselves. Listen now! Just before the darklings come, each of ye take a stone in your mouth and a twig of the witch-hazel in your hands, and go into the marshes without fear. Speak no word, for fear of your lives, but keep straight on till ye come to a spot where ye'll see a coffin with a cross and a candle on it. That's where ye'll find your Moon, I'm thinking, if ye're lucky.

So the next night as the dark began to fall they all trooped out into the marshes, each with a stone in his mouth and a twig of the witch-hazel in his hands. Never a word they spoke, but kept straight on; and, I'm telling you, there was not one among them but had the creeps and the starts. They could see nothing around them but bogs and pools and snags; but strange sighing whispers brushed past their ears, and cold wet hands sought theirs and tugged at the hazel twigs. But all at once, while looking everywhere for the coffin with the cross and the candle, they espied the big, strange stone, and it looked just like a coffin; while at the head of it was a black cross formed by the branches of the snag, and on this cross flickered a tiny light just like a candle.

When they saw these things they all knew that what the Wise Woman had told them was true: they were not far from their beloved Moon. But, being mighty feared of Bogles and the other Evil Things, they all went down on their knees in the mud and said the Lord's Prayer, once forwards, in keeping with the cross, and once backwards to keep off the Horrors of the Darkness. All this they said in their minds, without saying a word aloud, for they well knew what would happen to them if they neglected the Wise Woman's advice.

Then they rose up and laid hands on the great stone and heaved it up. And my Granny says, that as they did it, some of them saw, just for one tiddy-widdy little waste of a minute, the most beautiful face in the world gazing up at them with wistful eyes like—like— I really can't remember how my Granny described them, but it was either 'pools of gratitude' or 'lakes of love.' At all events, this is exactly what happened when the stone was rolled right over, and it was said so quickly that not one of them could describe it afterwards: 'Thanks, brave folk! I shall never forget your kindness,' as the Moon stepped up out of the black pool into her place in the sky.

Then they were all astonished beyond words, for, suddenly, all around was the silver light, making the safe ways between the bogs as clear as day. There was a sudden rush of weird things to their lairs, and then all was still and bright. Looking up, they saw with delight the full Moon sailing in the sky and smiling down upon them. She was there to light them home again. She was there to stampede the Evil Things—the Bogles and the Bad Little People —back into their vile dens. And, as the people looked around and wondered, it almost seemed to them that this time she had killed the Horrors dead—never to come to life again.

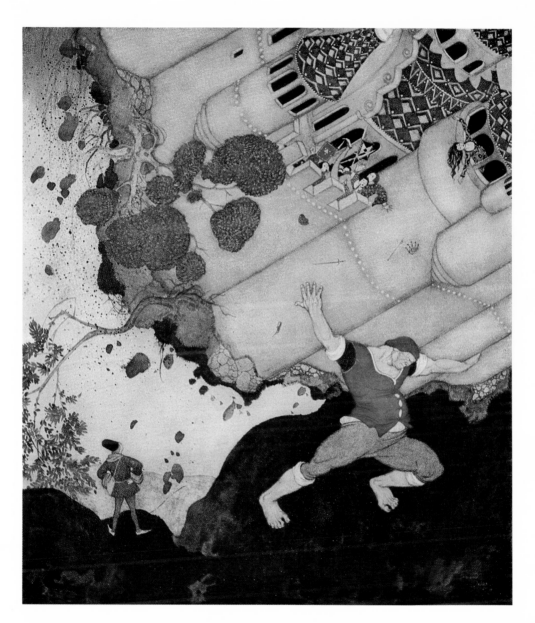

THE SEVEN CONQUERORS OF THE QUEEN
OF THE MISSISSIPPI

"'Hi! friend! Take the whole castle, with the Queen
and all that it contains, on your shoulders.'"

Page 29

THE SERPENT PRINCE

"When Grannmia saw her strange lover, she alone remained
calm and courageous."

Page 39

THE SEVEN CONQUERORS OF THE QUEEN
OF THE MISSISSIPPI

A BELGIAN FAIRY TALE

ONCE upon a time there was a boy who was ambitious.   One day he said to his mother: 'Give me a muffin and patch my trousers, for I am going to set out to win the Queen of the Mississippi.'

So the mother gave him a muffin and patched his trousers, and the boy went off.

He had not gone very far when he came to a mountain path, on which was a great cross, beneath which stood a man holding a bow with an arrow fixed on the string.

This man looked down at the boy as if to say, 'What are you doing here?'

The boy immediately answered his unspoken question by demanding, 'Hello, friend!   What are you doing there?'

'You see that fly on that cross?' said the man, pointing to a minute speck on one of its arms.   'Wait then, and watch me!   I will put out one of its eyes.'

With this, while the boy watched, he drew his bow to the full, and let the arrow fly.

It was a wonderful shot, for one of the eyes of the fly fell on the ground at the foot of the cross.

The boy was so taken with this, that he seemed to grow two whole years in half a minute.   To look at him, you would have thought he was no longer a boy.   He drew himself up proudly to his full height, and said in the voice of a young man:

'Will you travel with me, my pippy?'

'Pardon?'

Then it was question and answer between them :

' Come, travel with me, my pippy.'
' Oh ! Whither away ? To old Mandalay ?'
' But no ; to the far Mississippi,
Where a beautiful Queen holds sway :
And I 'll marry that Queen some day.'
' I am yours ! And the bounty ?'
' Give it a name : I will pay.'

Then the young man took his muffin, and, breaking off a little bit of it, handed it to the man with the bow and arrow.

' Keep it,' said he ; ' it 's a pledge of good faith.'

So they journeyed on together. When they had gone some distance, they came to a high field, and in the middle of this stood a man stock still, gazing at the sun. As soon as the young man saw him, he shouted out at the top of his voice : ' Hi ! What are you doing there, my good fellow ?'

' I am just waiting for it to get a little more dazzling,' replied the man, still keeping his eyes fixed on the midday sun.

As soon as the young man heard this he seemed to grow still more in stature. Indeed, he seemed to be almost a man.

' Will you travel with me ?' he said.

' Pardon ?'

Then it was question and answer between them :

' Come, travel with me, my pippy.'
' Oh ! Whither away ? To the land of Cathay ?'
' But no ; to the far Mississippi,
Where a beautiful Queen hath sway,
Who has stolen my heart away.'
' I am yours ! And the bounty ?'
' What you will : it 's a pleasure to pay.'

Then the young man took his muffin, and, breaking off a little bit of it, handed it to the man who gazed at the sun.

' Keep it,' said he ; ' it 's a pledge of good faith.'

So they journeyed on together.

When they had gone some distance further, they saw a man who had tied his legs together.

'Hello! What are you doing there, my friend?'

'I want to catch that hare over yonder; but unless I tied my legs together there would be no sport in it.'

'Will you travel with me?'

'Pardon?'

> '*Will you travel with me, my pippy?*'
>> '*Oh! Whither away? To Botany Bay?*'
> '*But no; to the far Mississippi,*
>> *Where a Queen—tooral-ooral-i-ay—*
>> *Is waiting for what I'm to say.*'
> '*I am yours! And the bounty?*'
>> '*Either here or in Botany Bay!*'

Then the boy took his muffin, and, breaking off a little piece, handed it to him.

'Keep it,' said he; 'it's a pledge of good faith.'

So they journeyed on together. But they had travelled scarce a league when they met a man who was carrying ten great trees in his arms. And when the boy, who had grown into a young man, saw this, he was immediately full grown.

'Hi! my friend! What are you doing there?'

'My mother wants some wood,' replied the man, picking a few branches off the trees and flinging them idly on the roadside, 'so I am just taking her some.'

'Will you travel with me?'

'Pardon?'

> '*Will you travel with me, my pippy?*'
>> '*Oh! Whither away? To Rome or Pompeii?*'
> '*But no; to the far Mississippi:*
>> *There's a Queen of great beauty that way,*
>> *And there's no one but Cupid to pay.*'
> '*I am yours! And the bounty?*'
>> '*Name your price: it shall be as you say.*'

Then the young man took his muffin, and, breaking off a little bit of it, handed it to the man who carried the trees.

'Keep it,' said he; 'it's a pledge of good faith.'

So they journeyed on together. They were still a long way from the Mississippi when they came across a man with a mouth large enough to swallow a river. When the boy, who had become a young man and was now full grown, set his eyes on him, his beard and moustache began to sprout.

'Will you travel with me?'

'Pardon?'

> *'Come, travel with me, my pippy.*
> *(Sing merry-ton-ton-ta-lay.)*
> *To the land of the far Mississippi*
> *Where the crystalline fountains play;*
> *There's a Queen who will not say me nay.'*
> *'I am yours! But the bounty?'*
> *'We're picking it up on the way.'*

Then the young man took his muffin, and, breaking off a little bit of it, handed it to the man with the mouth as large as a river.

'Keep it,' said he; 'it's a pledge of good faith.'

So they journeyed on together. On and on they went until at last they came to a great hill-top, and there, standing on the crest of it, they looked down into an immense valley where they saw a man engaged in eating up the whole earth. As soon as he saw this gigantic meal going on, the boy, who had become a young man and was now full grown with moustache and beard, appeared like a knight errant. One could see that, from the spurs which had grown upon his heels.

'Hi! What are you doing there?'

'I am so terribly hungry that nothing less than the whole earth can appease my appetite.'

'Will you travel with me?'

THE QUEEN OF THE MISSISSIPPI

'Pardon?'

> '*Come, travel with me, my pippy.*'
>   '*Oh! Whither?   Madras or Bombay?*'
> '*But no; to that far Mississippi,*
>   *Which flows from the gates of the day;*
>   *Where a Queen all in purple array*
>   *Waits for me——*'
> '*I am yours!   And the bounty?*'
>   '*Wouldn't go in a twenty-ton dray!*'

Then the young man took his muffin, and, breaking off a little bit, handed it to the man who was eating up the earth.

'Keep it,' said he; 'it's a pledge of good faith.'

They were still a long way from their destination when they came to a beautiful castle of burnished gold, surrounded by a very deep moat over which was a drawbridge; and on the bridge was a golden portcullis.   As soon as they arrived, their leader rang the bell.   When the door was opened, the travellers entered, and the hero asked to see the King.

'What do you want with the King?' replied an attendant, richly attired.

'I have come to ask for the hand of his daughter, the Queen of the Mississippi,' said the hero.

'That is all very well; but consider well before you start on such an undertaking; for many have come as you have come and have lost their lives.'

'That is nothing,' they all replied.   'We are not afraid!'

Then they were led before the Queen, and all were completely dazzled by her beauty.   It was a long time before they realised that she was speaking to them.   At last they understood her to say:

'Here is my servant.   See if you can eat more than he does.'

And the servant sat down in front of a table covered with dishes crowded with large joints of meat.   And behold, he ate the whole lot up.

'Oh! that is nothing at all,' said the young hero. And, turning to the man who ate up the earth, he said:

'Sit down there, my friend.' Then turning again to the servant, he ordered him to bring in the biggest bull they could find.

They obeyed, and set it down in front of the man who ate the earth. And, in presence of the Queen, he swallowed the bull whole, head and tail and everything; and it was alive!

But the Queen said, 'You have not won me yet!'

And then she called in a second servant and said:

'Here is my servant. See if you can drink more than he can!'

And immediately the servant took hold of a whole cask of wine, and in one mouthful drank the whole lot up.

The young hero said, 'That is nothing at all!' Then, turning to the man with a mouth as big as a river, he added:

'Come here, my friend. Place yourself on your stomach on the moat, and drink well!'

And the man with the mouth as large as a river placed himself on his stomach, with his mouth to the water of the great moat outside, and in one second he had drunk up the whole moat, fishes and all, absolutely dry.

But the Queen still said they had not won her!

And she beckoned another servant. Then, turning to the young man, she said: 'See if you can run better than he can. There,' she said, 'at the top of that high mountain, just near the sun, lives a hermit. Go and ask him what it is he wishes to say to me. Then come back and tell me.'

'Oh! that is nothing at all,' said the young hero. And, turning to the man who ran like a hare, he said: 'Go to the top of the mountain and come back with the message.'

And the man who ran like a hare was out of sight in a second, and before they could count three he had returned to the Queen with the message that the hermit was dead, which the Queen had known all the time.

And the young man said to the King:

THE QUEEN OF THE MISSISSIPPI

'You have submitted us to the test, and we have carried out all that you wished: we have now gained the Queen, and I am going to take her.'

Then the King got very angry and called out all his soldiers.

The young man, hearing this, said to the man with the strong arms:

'Hi! friend! Take the whole castle, with the Queen and all that it contains, on your shoulders!'

The man obeyed and they went on their way!

They had not gone a great distance when the man who had gazed at the sun cried out:

'In the distance I can see that we are being pursued by an army; they want to take the Queen!'

The King and his army approached rapidly, and demanded the Queen.

Then the man of the strong arm killed the King and every one of his army with a single blow.

Then he departed with the Queen and the castle to the home of the young man; and as soon as they got there the hero married the Queen, and, with her and his mother, they lived very happily to a good old age.

THE SERPENT PRINCE

AN ITALIAN FAIRY TALE

ONCE, a very long time ago, before aeroplanes emulated eagles and motor cars ran along swifter than the foxes, there lived on the outskirts of a great forest an old couple who were poor and childless and lonely.

Matteo was the name of this worthy pair, and the old man was called Cola and his wife was known as Sapatella. Now Matteo was a forester, and, because his duties kept him roaming from early morn until late in the evening through the deep dark glades of the forest, his wife, who had to stay at home and mind the cottage and prepare the meals, and never go out, not even to see the pictures on Saturday evenings, was very lonely indeed and wished more than ever that she had a son, so that *he* could go to the pictures and tell her all about them when he came home.

But wishes do not make horses or sons, nor even daughters, and so this poor old woman had to live a very lonely life indeed, which gave her a great deal of time to think and to envy

> *The old woman who lived in a shoe,*
> *Who had so many children she didn't know what to do,*

who lived about the same time in another part of the country.

One evening, when the days were growing short and the nights were correspondingly long and chilly, Matteo was on his way back to the cottage, when he remembered that Sapatella had asked him to bring home some faggots with him to cook with and to keep them warm, because, of course, when you are a forester and live in a forest,

31

you cannot expect to have coal to burn in your grates, like those who live in towns and villages.

There was plenty of brushwood, and heaps of twigs and fallen boughs lying about, and, as he had his axe with him, which all good foresters carry to clear a path for themselves through the dense undergrowths, it was not long before Matteo had collected a great bundle of faggots which was just as much as he could carry on his back.

But Matteo carried home with him on his back more than a mere bundle of dry boughs and twigs, although he did not know it. Neither did Sapatella, not until the next morning after Matteo had gone off to his work, when she went to the wood pile to get some sticks to put under her pot to boil the nice rabbit which Matteo had shot for her the day before. She picked up a bundle and was about to place it on the fire when a tiny serpent, oh, ever so tiny! slithered and wriggled its way out of the twigs and coiled itself up on the rug.

Being a forester's wife, Sapatella was not the least bit frightened of serpents or mice or beetles or other dreadful beasts; besides, it was such a tiny serpent, all yellow as can be; and, when the firelight danced on it, it shone bright and gleaming like gold.

'Ah me,' said the good woman with a sigh, 'even the serpents have their young ones, but I have no one.'

Then the serpent uncoiled and stretched itself out towards her and spoke. All kinds of animals spoke in those days, as you will notice if you read the story through, though not so frequently but that the good woman was surprised and startled to hear it.

'You may have me for your child if you will,' it said.

> '*Keep me warm and feed me well,*
> *And fortune will upon you dwell.*'

Sapatella was, as I have already said, considerably startled to hear a baby serpent talk like that; but she was a kind-hearted woman and very, very lonely, and she quickly made up her mind to adopt the little serpent and bring it up as her own.

THE SERPENT PRINCE

The forester, her husband, who was also kind-hearted, agreed to let her have her own way in the matter, and so the little serpent found a home and care and affection.

They kept him warm and fed him well,
And fortune did upon them dwell.

From that time on, peace and contentment and prosperity brightened the little cottage. Everything went smoothly and comfortably, though whether the little serpent had really anything to do with it or not, I cannot say.

Serpents grow up very quickly, and, what with the warmth and the good food and the affection, the little serpent soon grew to be a big one, oh, monstrous big! so that when he lay in front of the fire he took up the whole of the rug, and Sapatella had to scold him in order to make room so that she could attend to her cooking.

One day when she had nearly tripped over his tail and fallen with a pot of boiling water in her hands, Sapatella said to it: 'You are grown too big to be lying about before the fire all day. You must get up and do something.'

'Very well, mother,' said the serpent—it always called her mother, and Cola it called father, just as a son would. 'Find me a wife and I will get married and settle down.'

Sapatella did not very well know how to set about finding a wife for a serpent, even an adopted one; but she agreed to speak to Matteo her husband about the matter when he came home that night.

After supper, accordingly, she put the serpent's request to the forester.

'Our serpent wants to get married, Cola,' she said; 'so you must find him a wife.'

'Very well,' said Matteo. 'I will hunt through the forest when I am out, and try and find another serpent for him to mate with.'

'Oh, that will not do at all,' said the serpent, who had been listening very intently to its adopted parents' conversation, though it seemed to be sleeping peacefully all over the floor in front of the fire. 'I do not mate with serpents. You must get the King's daughter for me. To-morrow you must set out to the palace, and tell the King that I require his daughter in marriage.'

Naturally Matteo did not at all care about his errand; but his wife entreated him to go, and so on the morrow the good man set forth, the serpent watching him depart from the cottage door, chanting all the while:

> '*To the King my message tell,*
> *And fortune will upon you dwell.*'

Well, Matteo walked along through the forest on his way to the King's palace, and the nearer he got to his journey's end the more difficult and dangerous his errand seemed to grow. He thought the King would be sure to be very angry, and he might even order him to be hanged for a knave, or beaten off the palace grounds for a fool.

But he kept thinking of what the serpent had said, and, as good fortune dwelling upon us is something we all like to have, the forester kept on his way and resolved faithfully to carry out his errand.

He came at last to the palace gates, and as, in those days, in that country, any one who wanted to could walk in and speak to the King, this simple old fellow passed in with the crowd who were going to seek help or justice, and in due time he came before the King.

'O great King!' he said, 'a serpent who is my adopted son has sent me to ask your daughter's hand in marriage.'

The King stared, and then he frowned, and then he stared again. Kings are accustomed to receiving strange requests; but never anything so strange as this.

Fortunately for Cola, the King was a good-humoured, easy-going man, and, thinking that he had to do with some harmless old lunatic, he only laughed, as did all the courtiers and people who stood about him.

'Very well,' he said. 'I will grant your request, only your adopted son must first of all turn all the fruit in my orchard into gold. Then will I give him my daughter in marriage.'

Matteo thanked the King for his great clemency and kindness in not having him hanged or beaten out of the palace, and then started off home again.

'I am well out of that,' he thought to himself; 'but my adopted son will have to be contented with a wife of less degree. Who ever heard of turning apples and flowers and cherries into gold? Why, they can only make copper and silver of them in Covent Garden.'

But the serpent didn't seem in the least bit concerned when the forester told him the result of his errand.

'That is a small matter,' it said. 'To-morrow morning you must go into the city with a basket, and gather up all the fruit-stones you can find, and take them and scatter them in the orchard.

'Do this thing and do it well,
And fortune will upon you dwell.'

So Matteo went once more to the town and did exactly as the serpent had told him. Not knowing anything of magic, he did not in the least expect anything to happen; so you may imagine his surprise when not only the fruit, but every tree and leaf and bough in the whole orchard, turned into solid gold, and glittered so in the sunlight that one could scarcely bear to look at them.

It chanced that the King was walking on the terrace with his courtiers when Matteo entered the orchard.

'There is that silly old man come back again who wants me to wed my daughter to a serpent,' he said. 'Is he going to turn my fruit into gold by stealing it and selling it in the market-place?'

The courtiers laughed at this excellent jest, as courtiers will; but the next moment they stopped laughing, and each one rubbed his eyes and ejaculated in astonishment and delight at the marvellous beauty and value of the King's orchards.

The King himself could say nothing, and he said nothing, until

35

Matteo came before him and humbly begged his Majesty to fulfil his promise now that the serpent, his adopted son, had done the task assigned to him.

The King was in a quandary. He was not greedy or avaricious; but to have a serpent for a son-in-law was, for a king, clearly impossible.

'Softly,' he said. 'You have fulfilled your task, it is true; but so fair an orchard requires a better setting. Golden trees should not grow out of common ground and be enclosed by common walls. Let your adopted son first turn all the ground and the walls into diamonds and rubies and precious stones, so that I may have orchards whereof the like is not known in all the world, and then will I give him my daughter to wife.'

The forester again thanked his Majesty for his great condescension and retired, while the King and his courtiers went into the orchard and picked golden apples and plums and peaches from golden boughs, and marvelled at the wonderful thing that had been done before their eyes.

It was in the King's mind that this could be no common or forest serpent, and he was troubled to think what his position would be if the second task was performed as readily and thoroughly as the first had been.

When Matteo reached home and told the serpent what had befallen him, the serpent shook his tail and seemed about to fly into a passion.

'You see how well kings keep their word,' it said angrily. 'But it is a small matter after all. Do you go again to the town on the morrow, and gather all the broken bits of china and glass you can find. These you must take in a basket, and lay a piece on each wall and between each tree and bush.

'Do this thing and do it well,
And fortune will upon you dwell.'

So Matteo set out at daybreak, and did exactly as the serpent had told him. He had no difficulty in finding plenty of material for his purpose, and it was still early when he reached the orchard with a heavy load of broken tea-cups and plates and oddments of basins and teapots and water-jugs.

Early as it was, it was not too early for the King to be present. The wonder of this new possession had kept his Majesty awake nearly all night, and he was impatient until he could get into the orchard and satisfy himself that it was all really and actually true.

When he saw Matteo approach and lay down his fragments of china, he grew thoughtful, for he realised that it was all true enough, and that the second condition would be likely to be performed. But he said nothing, and Matteo walked from tree to tree, dropping here a piece of cup, there a fragment of plate; and, wherever the china fell, the ground between the trees turned to diamond or sapphire or ruby. With the walls it was just the same. Every kind of precious stone known and unknown was to be found in that wonderful orchard, even to a carbuncle which grew on a courtier's toe in consequence of his incautious action in putting his foot just where Matteo was dropping a tiny bit of china.

The King was delighted and depressed at the same time. He had got orchards surpassing in beauty and value anything that was known to be in the whole world; also he had to give his daughter in marriage to a serpent, and the last seemed to the poor King of greater consideration than the former.

'Tell the serpent, your adopted son, that, although he has accomplished the task I set him, yet will I not give him my daughter to wed unless he also turns my palace into gold,' he said to Matteo, and again the forester thanked the King for his great clemency and condescension, and returned to his home.

Again the serpent grew angry and said shrewd things concerning the value of the word of kings, and the trust which is not to be found in princes—not even German princes.

'But,' said he, 'it is a small matter. Do you go at daybreak and gather in the forest herbs of this kind and that, and make them into a broom, and sweep therewith the whole length of the palace walls, and so shall it be even as the King wishes.

'Go do this thing and do it well,
And fortune shall upon you dwell.'

So Matteo went into the forest and gathered herbs of this kind and that, and swept the palace well round as the serpent had directed, and when the King and his courtiers and the servants—even down to the scullery wench—arose, the whole palace was golden from the front step of the main entrance to the topmost ridge of the chimney. And it was not gold plate either: it was all solid gold of the purest kind.

This time the King saw that there was no way of escape when Matteo asked for the fulfilment of the royal promise, so he called his daughter to him and told her of the matter.

'My dear Grannmia,' he said, for that was her name, 'for your sake I have twice broken my royal pledge, and now I greatly fear you must keep it. It is a small matter—just to marry a serpent, the adopted son of a poor forester.'

The Princess, who was very young and very dutiful, and surpassingly fair to look upon, agreed cheerfully, as though marrying serpents was quite an ordinary everyday duty like laying foundation stones and receiving bouquets.

So the King told Matteo to send the serpent along and marry his daughter, and for goodness' sake not to bother him any further with golden palaces, and jewelled orchards, and carbuncles on his favourite courtier's big toe.

When the serpent heard this from Matteo, it seemed beside itself with joy, and there and then set off for the palace. But before it left the humble cottage in which it had received so much care and affection, it bade farewell to Sapatella and Matteo, and thanked them very heartily for all their goodness, finishing up with these words:

'Now my task you have done full well,
Good fortune shall upon you dwell.'

38

And it did; for, from that time till the day they died, both Sapatella and Matteo were happy and contented and prosperous, and never ailed or suffered pain or disappointment.

When Grannmia saw her strange lover, she alone remained calm and courageous—the only one in the palace who did. All the servants ran shrieking when they saw the great golden monster entering the doors, and, when it got to the presence-chamber, the King and Queen fled in one direction and the courtiers in another. Only the Princess remained, trembling with astonishment, and awaited the pleasure of the serpent.

Slowly it came gliding towards her, and then, when it was almost near enough for her to touch it, it reared up—the golden skin fell apart, and a young and most handsome Prince stood bowing before her.

Now, of course, everything would have been happy and joyous if it had not been for the silly old King, who, partly out of anxiety for his daughter, but chiefly from curiosity, stole back and peeped into the room just as the Prince emerged from the golden skin which had disguised him as a serpent.

He did just what you should never do with disenchanted princes: rushed forward and threw the discarded skin into the fire, where it flashed and burned like a resinous torch.

At the sound of the crackling the Prince turned, and, when he saw what had happened, he was furiously angry, more angry, in fact, than he had been when, as a serpent, he had reflected on the unreliability of the promises of kings. Then, with a sad look at the Princess, he turned to the King and said:

> *' This act of yours renews the spell,*
> *May fortune never with you dwell.'*

And, turning himself into a dove, he circled three times round the Princess and then flew through the window. At least, he would have flown through the window, only it did not happen to be open. In consequence he broke the pane and very nearly his own head; but he got out, and flew straight away over the golden orchard, while the Princess, who had rushed to the window, stood gazing after him until he could no longer be seen. Then she turned and gave the unhappy King her views of his meddlesome prying. Then she burst into tears and cried until the sun went down, so that the tears formed a stream and ran down into the fountain-court, and all the poor little goldfish died because of too much salt in their fresh water.

But crying does not help any one, so, after all the palace servants had gone to bed, she gathered up all her treasures and set out to find her elusive husband, who had come to her as a serpent with a wriggly tail, and flown away as a dove with a bit of a broken window-pane in his head.

When she got out of the palace grounds into the woods behind, she met a fox who was also looking for a dove, or a fowl, or any other winged thing.

The fox said, 'Good evening, pretty Princess. May I travel with you for company?'

'Yes, do,' said the Princess. 'I am not used to the woods at night, and I may not be able to find my way.'

So the fox led her through the wood and far away from the palace until they had gone miles and miles, and the Princess was so tired that she would not go another step, not even to find a dove with a bandaged head. So they both lay down and went to sleep.

It was late in the morning when she awoke and heard the birds singing all around her.

Their song pleased her very much, and the fox, noticing this, remarked: 'Ah, if you could only understand what they are saying you would be much more pleased.'

'Oh, do tell me, dear fox,' pleaded the Princess; and, after he had made her ask him a sufficient number of times, the fox replied:

'Well, they are saying that the King's son, who was turned into a serpent by his godmother to spite his father, has met with an accident that now threatens his life. The spell lasted for seven years, and, on the very day it ended, he was about to marry the daughter of another king, when her father rashly burnt the skin and thus caused him to be turned into a dove. In flying from the palace he has cut his head against a window-pane, and is now at his father's palace lying so sadly hurt that none of the doctors can do anything for him.'

The Princess was greatly concerned at hearing this story.

'But listen, dear fox, and hear if the birds say whether there is any way of curing this poor Prince,' she said.

So the fox listened intently, and by and by he said to the Princess: 'The blackbirds are saying there is no way, but the wrens say there is one. Whoever would cure the Prince must obtain the blood from these very birds and pour it on the head of the Prince, when he will immediately recover and be as well as he ever was.'

The Princess began to grow hopeful, and begged of the fox to catch the birds for her so that she might obtain the remedy and restore the Prince to health. She added a promise of reward for his assistance, and the fox agreed to help her.

So they waited under the trees until the sun had gone in and the birds were all asleep in their nests, and then the fox climbed stealthily into the trees and gathered the birds one after the other, just like a naughty schoolboy stealing apples from a farmer's orchard.

Having obtained what she required, the Princess set forth eagerly to carry the remedy to the Prince's palace.

But the fox, who had taken care to keep well out of her reach, suddenly sat down and began to laugh.

'Why do you laugh, dear fox?' asked the Princess. 'Is it that you are overjoyed to think that the Prince who is to be my husband will soon be restored to health? But let us hurry: we may be too late!'

'No, it is not that,' said the fox, laughing again. 'It is to think that your remedy will be of no avail without the other ingredient, which is the blood of a fox, and as I am not minded to supply it, I will skip the reward you promised and be off.'

Thereupon he started away, pelting*as hard as he could go.

The Princess saw that her only hope was to outwit the fox, and she immediately thought of a plan to gain her end.

'Dear fox, do not run,' she said; 'that would be a pity now that the remedy is in our own hands. The King is certain to reward us lavishly, and surely there are plenty of other foxes among whom we can find one willing to spare his blood to save the King's son. Let us go on, then, and trust to our fortune.'

The fox, proud of the fact of being the most artful animal alive, never thought for one moment that he could be exceeded in cunning by a simple maiden, so he came back to the Princess, and together they walked through the forest to the far end where the palace of the King showed in the near distance.

'That is the place,' said the fox; 'but we haven't got the other ingredient!'

'Oh yes, we have,' said the Princess, and, before the fox could be any more artful, she hit him on the head with a stout branch she had picked up, and with such force that he did not in the least object to the necessary addition to the Prince's medicine being drawn from his own veins.

Of course the Princess was sorry to have to do this. The fox had helped her a great deal; and besides, she was a tender-hearted little thing, and she wept like anything all the while she was compounding the remedy; but princes are of more importance than foxes, particularly when they are handsome princes who have been serpents and are wanted to make handsome husbands.

So the Princess took the phial containing the very strange cure for wounded heads, and proceeded straight to the King's palace.

They were all so disturbed, with the servants running about distractedly, and the doctors quarrelling with each other, and the courtiers standing about trying not to look bored, that no one took the least notice of the Princess; but she was a pushing young lady, and seeing the palace doors all open, she made her way from room to room until at last she found the King himself.

42

Pelting, rushing

THE SERPENT PRINCE

'And it please your Majesty,' she said, dropping him a curtsy, 'I have come to save the Prince.'

'But how can you save the Prince when all the great doctors in my kingdom cannot?' demanded the King.

> '*The birds told me,*
> *The fox helped me,*
> *And I can save your son.*
> *But, if I do, I ask of you*
> *To marry me to him when I've done,*'

chanted the Princess.

The King was so overcome with grief and anxiety that he was ready to promise anything to anybody who could help him, so he gave the Princess the required promise, and, without more ado, she caused herself to be led into the chamber of the Prince, and poured the contents of the phial over his wound.

The Prince, who had been so nearly at the point of death that no one would have believed to see him that there was any life in him at all, immediately sat up, recovered and well.

He did not recognise the Princess, and when the King, his father, told him the terms on which she had saved his life, and presented the maiden to him, he refused.

'For the great service you have rendered me I am grateful indeed,' he said; 'but I cannot marry you. My heart is already given to another, and not even for my life will I be false to my word.'

When she heard this the Princess was secretly overjoyed; but she pretended to be greatly displeased, and she disdainfully rejected all other offers of reward that were made to her by the King and the Prince.

'Tell me who this other is, and I will go to her and get her to relinquish you in my favour,' she said at length. 'When she learns what I have done for you, I am sure she will agree that my claim is greater than hers.'

'It is the Princess Grannmia; but that I am sure she will never do,' said the Prince proudly. 'Even if she would, I will not. What is life without love? and I would rather be a serpent again, and live in the cottage of a poor forester all my days, than rule this kingdom without my beloved Princess.'

On hearing this the Princess could no longer keep her secret.

'You must love me indeed, dear Prince,' she said, 'if you do not recognise me when I come pleading to you to carry out your promise after saving your life, and marry me as you would have done when the King, my father, drove you away from me.'

Then the Prince recognised her, and he embraced her so heartily that the Princess wondered whether he was still a serpent or only just a strong young man who was very much in love with her, while the King went out and gave immediate orders to set the bells a-ringing, and have preparations made on the most lavish scale for the wedding feast.

THE HIND OF THE WOOD

A FRENCH FAIRY TALE

ONCE upon a time there lived a King and a Queen whose marriage was as happy as happy could be; they loved each other tenderly, and, in turn, their subjects loved them; but one thing clouded their life: and that was that they had no children, no heir. The Queen thought that the King would love her much more if she had a child. So she made up her mind to drink of the water of a certain spring. People came there in thousands from afar to drink of this special kind of water; and one saw so many that it looked as though all the world and his wife were there.

Now there were many, many lovely fountains in the wood where the Queen and other people went to drink at the spring; so the Queen asked her ladies to lead the others away to these fountains to amuse themselves, and leave her alone. Then, when they had all withdrawn, she bewailed in a plaintive voice.

'Am I not unhappy,' she said, 'to have no children! The poor women, who can badly afford them, have plenty; but here it is now five years that I have begged heaven to give me one. Oh! am I to die without ever having a little child? Never! Never! Nev——'

She broke off suddenly, for she saw that the water of the fountain was troubled. Then a big Crayfish came up and climbed on to the bank and spoke to her:

'Great Queen, you shall have your desire. Near here is the grand palace which the fairies built, but it is impossible for you to find it, because it is surrounded by strong fairy barricades, through which no mortal eye could ever see, nor mortal footstep pass without

45

a guide. But I am your humble servant, and, if you will trust your-self to me, I will take you there.'

The Queen listened without interrupting, for hearing a big Crayfish talk—and talk so nicely too—was a great surprise to her. But there was a still greater surprise in store. The Crayfish waved its feelers in the air, and, before she could count three, it had taken the form of a beautiful little old woman, with pretty snow-white hair and a dainty shepherdess costume. She bowed low, and then spoke.

'Well, madam,' said she, 'always look upon me as one of your friends, for I wish nothing but what would be for your good.'

She was so sweet and charming that the Queen kissed her, and then by common consent they went off hand in hand through the wood by a way which surprised the Queen.

It was the way by which the fairies came from the palace to the fountains. As they went the Queen paused to look at a strange thing which made her heart beat very fast. At a certain spot the bushes overhead were full of roses and orange blossoms, entwined and laced in such a way as to form a cradle covered with leaves. The earth beneath was a carpet of violets, and, in the giant cedars above, thousands of little birds, each one a different colour, sang their songs; and the meaning of their melody was this: that cradle, woven by fairy fingers, was not there for nothing.

The Queen had not got over this surprise before she saw in the distance a castle that dazzled her vision, so splendid did it shine. To tell the truth, the walls and the ceilings were of nothing but diamonds, and all the benches—even the balcony and terraces—all were pure diamonds scintillating with flashes beyond the strength of human eyes to bear. The Queen gave a great cry of joy as she covered her eyes with her hand. Then, as they came to the gate of the castle, she asked the little old woman if what she saw were real, or if she were dreaming?

'Nothing is more real, madam,' the fairy replied. And at that moment the door of the castle opened and six other fairies came out. But what fairies! They were the most beautiful ever seen. They all made a low bow to the Queen, and each one presented her with a branch flowering with petals of precious stones, to make herself a bouquet. One bore roses, another tulips, another rare wild-flowers, and the rest budded with carnations and pomegranates.

'Madam,' they said, 'we could not give you a greater mark of our friendship for you, than to invite you here. We are pleased to be able to tell you that you shall have a lovely little Princess whom you shall call Désirée. Be sure not to forget that, when she is born, you summon us, because we wish to endow her with all the good qualities possible. All you will have to do is to take the branches of the bouquet, and, in naming each flower, think of the fairy of that name; rest assured that we shall be in your room immediately.'

The Queen, full of joy, threw her arms around each one's neck in turn, and kissed them all, over and over again, for half an hour. After that they begged the Queen to go through their palace, and the diamonds were so bright that the Queen could not keep her eyes open. Then they took her through their garden. Never was there such lovely fruit; the apricots were larger than her head, and she could only eat a quarter of one, and the taste was so lovely that the Queen resolved never to eat anything else as long as she lived. She remained in the palace until the evening, and then, having thanked the fairies for all they had done for her, she returned with the Fairy of the Fountain.

Now, when the Queen went home, she found that they were all very upset, and had been searching for her, and could not think where she had gone. Some had thought that, as she was so beautiful and young, some stranger had taken her away: which was reasonable, for she spoke so nicely to every one. But now at last they had found her, and the King was himself again.

The Queen soon found that what the fairies had said was true. On a certain day she had a little daughter, and she called her Désirée. Then, remembering their words, she at once took the bouquet and named each flower and thought of the fairies one after the other, and lo! immediately they were all there. Their arms were crammed full of presents. And, after they had kissed the Queen and the little Princess, they began to distribute the presents. There was beautiful lace with the history of the world worked into it; then came a lovely cover all marked in gold representing all the toys that children play with. The cot was then shown, and the Queen went into raptures over it: it surely was the nicest ever made; it was of beautiful, rare wood, with a canopy of blue silk, inwrought with diamonds and rubies.

Then the fairies took the little Princess on their knees, and kissed her and hugged her because she was so good and beautiful. Each fairy wished her a good quality. One wished her to be wise; another wished that she might be good; another wished her to be virtuous; another to be beautiful; another to possess a good fortune; and the fifth asked for her a long life and good health. Then came the last, and she wished that Désirée might obtain all that she herself could ever wish for.

The Queen thanked them a hundred times for all the good things they had given her little daughter, and, while she was doing so, all gave a sudden start, for the door opened and a tremendous Crayfish—so large that it could hardly get through the door—came in, waving its feelers in the air.

'O ungrateful Queen!' said the Crayfish, 'you did not trouble to ask me here. Is it possible that you have so soon forgotten the Fairy of the Fountain and the good services I did in taking you to my sisters. Why, you have invited all of them, and I am the only one forgotten.'

The Queen was terribly upset at her error, and begged the Fairy to forgive her. She hastened to assure her that she had not for a moment forgotten her great obligation to her; and she begged her not to go back on her friendship, and particularly to be good to the little Princess.

The others thought that the Fairy of the Fountain would wish evil to the baby Princess, so they said to her: 'Dear sister, do not be cross with the Queen; she is good and never would offend you.'

THE HIND OF THE WOOD

Now, as the Fairy of the Fountain liked to be spoken to nicely, this softened her a little, and she said:

'Very well, I will not wish her all the harm I was going to; I will lessen it a little. But take care that she never sees the light of day until she is fifteen, or she and you will have reason to regret it. That is all I have to say.' Then, suddenly changing into the little old woman with the white hair and shepherdess dress, she pirouetted through the wall, staff in hand. And the cries of the Queen and the prayers of the good fairies did not matter a bit.

The Queen begged the other fairies to avert the terrible catastrophe, and besought them to tell her what to do. They consulted together, and at last told the Queen that they would build a palace without any windows or doors, and with an underground passage, so that the Princess's food could be brought to her. And she was to be kept there until she was fifteen.

Then, with a wave of their wands, they made a lovely, pure-white marble castle spring up, and, inside of this, all the chairs were made of jewels, and even the floors were no different. And here the little Princess dwelt and grew up a good and beautiful child, possessing all the good qualities that her fairy godmothers had wished for her; and from time to time they came to see how she was getting on. But, of all the fairy godmothers, Tulip was the favourite. She reminded the Queen never to forget the warning not to allow the Princess to see the light of day, lest the terrible fate that the Fairy of the Fountain had laid upon her would surely come to pass. The Queen, of course, promised never to forget so important a matter.

Now, just as her little daughter was nearing the age of fifteen, the Queen had her portrait taken and sent to all the great courts of the world. And so it happened that one Prince, when he saw it, took it and shut it up in his cabinet and talked to the portrait as though it was the Princess herself in the flesh.

The courtiers heard him and went and told his father that his son had gone mad, and that he was shut up in his room, talking all day long to something or somebody who wasn't there.

The King immediately sent for his son and told him what the courtiers had said about him; then he asked him if it was true, and what had come over him to act like this.

The Prince thought this a favourable opportunity, so he threw himself at the feet of the King and said:

'You have resolved, sire, to marry me to the Princess Maigre, but I love the Princess Désirée.'

'You have not seen her,' said the King. 'How can you love her?'

'Neither have I seen the Princess Maigre, but I have both their portraits,' replied the Warrior Prince (he was so named because he had won three great battles), 'but I assure you that I have such a love for the Princess Désirée, that if you do not withdraw your word to the Princess Maigre and allow me to have Désirée, I shall die, and I shall be very glad to do so if I am unable to have the Princess I love.'

'It is to her portrait, then, that you have been speaking?' said the King. 'My son, you have made yourself the laughing-stock of the whole court. They think you are mad.'

'You would be as much struck as I am if you saw her portrait,' replied the Prince firmly.

'Fetch it and show it to me, then,' said the King, equally firmly.

The Prince went, and returned with the Princess's portrait as requested; and the King was so struck with her beauty that he gave the Prince leave there and then to marry her, and promised to withdraw his word from the other Princess.

'My dear Warrior,' said he, 'I should love to have so beautiful a Princess in my court.'

The Prince kissed his father's hand and bowed his knee, for he could not conceal his joy. He begged the King to send a messenger not only to the Princess Maigre but also to Princess Désirée; and he hoped that in regard to his own Princess, he would choose a man who would prove the most capable; and he must be rich, because this was a special occasion and called for all the elaborate preparation it was possible to show in such a diplomatic mission.

THE HIND OF THE WOOD

The King's choice fell on Prince Becafigue; he was a young Prince who spoke eloquently, and he possessed five millions of money. And, beside this, he loved the Warrior Prince very dearly.

When the messenger was taking his leave the Prince said to him:

'Do not forget, my dear Becafigue, that my life depends on my marrying Princess Désirée, whom you are going to see. Do your best for me and tell the Princess that I love her.' Then he handed Becafigue his photograph to give the Princess.

The young Prince Becafigue's cortège was so grand, and consisted of so many carriages, that it took them twenty-three hours to pass; and the whole world turned out to see him enter the gates of the palace where the King and Queen and Princess Désirée lived. The King and Queen saw him coming and were very pleased with all his grandeur, and commanded that he should be received in a manner befitting so great a personage.

Becafigue was taken before the King and Queen, and, after paying his respects to them, told them his message and asked to be introduced to the Princess Désirée. What was his surprise on being refused!

'I am very sorry to have to say no to your request, Prince Becafigue,' said the King, 'but I will tell you why. On the day the Princess was born a fairy took an aversion to her, and said that a great misfortune should befall her if she saw the light of day before she was fifteen years of age.'

'And am I to return without her?' said Becafigue. 'Here is a portrait of the Warrior Prince.' Then, as he was handing it to the King, and was about to say something further about it, a voice came from the photograph, speaking with loving tones:

'Dear Désirée, you cannot imagine with what joy I wait for you: come soon to our court, where your beauty will grace it as no other court will ever be graced.'

The portrait said nothing more, and the King and the Queen were so surprised that they asked Becafigue to allow them to show it to the Princess.

Becafigue readily assented and the Queen took the portrait to the Princess and showed it to her; and the Princess was delighted. Although the Queen had told her nothing, the Princess knew that it meant a great marriage, and was not surprised when her mother asked: 'Would you be cross if you had to marry this man?'

'Madam,' said the Princess, 'it is not for me to choose; I shall be pleased to obey whatever you wish.'

'But,' said the Queen, 'if my choice should fall on this particular Prince, would you consider yourself happy?'

The Princess blushed and turned her eyes away and said nothing; then the Queen took her in her arms and kissed her, for she loved the Princess very much and knew that she would soon lose her, for it wanted only three months to her fifteenth birthday.

When the Prince knew that he could not have his dear Princess Désirée until three months had passed, he became very sad, and could not sleep at night, until at last his strength gave way and he was near to death. Doctors were called in, but they could do nothing at all, and the King was in a dreadful state, for he loved his son very much.

Now the other messenger, who was sent to the Princess Maigre to tell her that the Prince had changed his mind and was going to marry another, was admitted to her presence and soon explained his errand.

'Mr. Messenger,' she said when he had finished, 'is it possible that your master does not think I am beautiful or rich enough? Look out over my broad lands and you will find that they are so vast that you cannot see where they end; and, as for money, I have large coffers full to the brim, as any one will tell you.'

'Madam,' replied the messenger, 'I blame my master as much as a humble subject may. Now if I were sitting on the greatest throne in the world, I would think it the highest favour from heaven if you would share it with me.'

'That speech has saved your life,' said the Princess Maigre, 'you may go.'

THE HIND OF THE WOOD

When the Fairy of the Fountain heard this she was extremely angry and she looked in her book to make sure that the Warrior Prince had really left the Princess Maigre in favour of the Princess Désirée. Yes, it was quite true.

'What!' cried the Fairy of the Fountain, 'this ill-omened Désirée is always in some way upsetting my plans. No! I will not allow it to happen: why should I?'

Now the messenger Becafigue hurried along to the court of Désirée's father and mother, and threw himself at their feet, and told them that his master was very ill and likely to die if he did not see the Princess.

The King and Queen agreed that it would be best to go and tell the Princess about the Prince; so the Queen went and told her daughter all she knew, not forgetting to mention the evil wish that had been laid upon her at the time of her birth. But the Princess asked her mother if it were not possible to defeat this wish by taking steps to send her to the Prince in a carriage with all the light shut out.

This was agreed upon and a carriage was made on a subtle plan, with a separate compartment for the Princess, and mouse-trap blinds through which food and drink could be inserted without admitting the light of day. In this she, with her two ladies-in-waiting, Long-Epine and Giroflée, set forth, and all the court wept together with the King and Queen at the going away of their little Princess.

Now Long-Epine did not care for Désirée very much, and, what is more, she loved the Warrior Prince, having seen his photograph and heard him speak.

The Queen's last words at parting were:

'Take care of my little daughter, and do not on any account let her see the light of day. I have made all arrangements with the Prince that she is to be shut up in a room where she will not be able to see the light, and every care will be taken.' And, with these words in their ears, they set off, having promised the Queen that all would be done as she wished.

53

THE HIND OF THE WOOD

Long-Epine told herself she would never let the Princess win the Warrior Prince, not if she could prevent it; so, at dinner time that day, when the sun was at its highest, she went as usual to the carriage with the Princess's food, and, with a big knife, slit the blind so that the light streamed in. No sooner had she done so than a strange thing happened. The Princess had been quite alone in the darkened compartment; then how was it that a white hind leapt out through the window and sped away into the forest? Long-Epine watched it, wondering. Then she looked in at the window, but the compartment was empty. The Princess had gone!

Immediately the Princess, in the form of a white hind, had disappeared into the forest, her good friend Giroflée began to chase after her. As soon as she had gone, Long-Epine took the clothes of her mistress and dressed herself up in them, and resolved to impersonate the Princess before the young Prince. Then the carriage drove on, and in it sat Long-Epine disguised as the Princess.

When they arrived she presented herself as Désirée; but the Prince looked at her with horror, for she was not at all like a real Princess. Désirée's dress, which she wore, came to her knees, and she had not noticed that her ugly legs showed below the dress.

'This is not the Princess of the portrait,' said the Prince and his father together. 'You took us for fools, no doubt!'

The false Princess said that it was a terrible thing to bring her away from her kingdom to be treated in this way, and to break the word that they had given. 'How can you do this?' she cried.

At this the Prince and his father were so angry that they did not reply at all, but simply had the false Princess clapped in irons and put into prison.

The Prince was so heart-broken at this new trouble that he resolved to go and shut himself up for the remainder of his life, alone. At once he summoned the faithful Becafigue, and told him all. Then he wrote a letter to his father and sent it by Becafigue.

'If I never see my real Princess again,' he wrote, 'I beg of

THE HIND OF THE WOOD

"Girofle thanked the fairy and went...far into the wood;
and there, sure enough, she saw a hut and an old woman
sitting outside."

Page 56

IVAN AND THE CHESTNUT HORSE

"The chestnut horse seemed to linger in the air at the top
of its leap while that kiss endured."

Page 69

you that at least you will keep that sham one locked up, and guard her close.'

Now all this time the Princess was in the wood, running hither and thither as hinds do. Once or twice she looked at herself in the water of the fountain, and saw herself so changed that she cried out: 'Is it I? Am I this hind?' Then at last she got very hungry, and began to eat berries and herbs, and finally sought a quiet spot and went to sleep.

The Fairy Tulip had always loved the Princess, and said that if she left the castle before she was fifteen, she was sure that the Fairy of the Fountain would relent and do her no harm. But, as for Giroflée, she was all this time wandering round looking for the little Princess. She had walked so much and now felt so tired that she lay down and went to sleep in the forest. The next morning the Princess, seeking moss among the ferns, found her. When she saw that it was Giroflée, she went up to her and caressed her with her nozzle, as hinds do, and looked into her eyes until at last Giroflée knew full well that it was the Princess turned into a White Hind. She watched the Hind attentively and saw two large tears fall from her eyes, and then there was not a single doubt that it was her dear little Princess; so she put her arms around her neck, and they wept together.

Then Giroflée told the Princess that she would never leave her, and that she would stay with her until the end.

The Hind understood, and, to show her gratitude, took Giroflée into the very deepest part of the forest to find her some luscious fruit which she had seen there; but on the way Giroflée called out in alarm: she would die of fright if she had to spend the night in such a desolate spot; and then they both began to cry. Their cries were so pitiful that they touched the heart of the good Fairy Tulip, and she came to their aid.

Giroflée begged her to have pity on her young mistress, and to give her back her natural form, but the Fairy Tulip said that it was impossible to do that. She said that she would do what she could.

She told Giroflée that if she went into the forest, she would come to the hut of an old woman. She was to speak her fair and ask her to take charge of both of them. Then when night came, the Princess would change back into her natural form; but as this could only happen at night in the hut, they must be very careful.

Now Giroflée thanked the fairy and went, as she had told her, far into the wood; and there, sure enough, she saw a hut and an old woman sitting outside on a bench. She went up to her at once.

'My dear mother,' she said, 'will you allow me to have a little room in your house for myself and my little Hind?'

'Yes, my dear daughter,' she replied, 'I will certainly give you a room.' And she immediately took them into the hut, and then into the dearest little room it was possible to find. It contained two little beds all draped in pure white and beautifully clean.

As the night began to come in, Désirée changed her form and became the Princess again; and, seeing this, Giroflée kissed her and hugged her with delight. The old woman knocked at the door, and, without entering, she handed Giroflée some fresh fruit which they were very pleased to have to eat; and then they went to bed. But, as soon as day dawned, Désirée took again the shape and form of a White Hind.

Now Becafigue was in the very same wood, and came to the hut where the old woman lived. He begged her to give him something for his master to eat; but the old woman told him that if his master spent the night in the forest, harm would surely happen to him, because it was full of wild animals. Why should he not come to her hut? Why should he not accept the little room she could offer him? He was welcome to it and a good meal besides.

Then Becafigue went back and told the Prince all that the old woman had said and persuaded him to accept her offer. They put the Prince into the room next to the Princess, but neither of them knew anything of this arrangement.

The next morning the Prince called Becafigue, and told him that he was going into the forest and that he was not to follow him.

THE HIND OF THE WOOD

The Prince had walked and walked for a long time in the forest, grieving over his loss, when suddenly in the distance he saw a lovely little White Hind, and gave chase and tried to catch it. The Hind, who was no other than the little Princess, ran and ran far away until the Prince, in utter fatigue, gave up the chase; but he resolved to look again the next day, and to be more careful this time, so as not to let the Hind get away. Then he went home and told the story to Becafigue, while the Princess on her side was telling her dear Giroflée that a young hunter had chased her and tried to kill her, but she was so fleet-footed that she got away.

Giroflée told her not to go out any more, but to stay in and read some books that she would find for her; but, after a little thought, the Princess found it too awful to be shut up in one little room all day long, so the next morning she went out again into the forest, and wandered through the beautiful dells and glades. After going some distance she saw a young hunter lying down on the mossy bank asleep, and, approaching him cautiously, she found that she was now so very close to him that it would be impossible to get away before he awoke. Then again, he was so handsome, that, instead of running away, she rubbed her little nose against the young hunter. What was her surprise to see that it was her dear Prince! for he, at her caress, opened his eyes, and she at once recognised him. And when he jumped up and stroked and patted her, she trembled with delight and raised her beautiful eyes to his in the dumb eloquence of love.

'Ah! little White Hind,' said he, 'if you only knew how miserable I am, and what the cause of it is, you would not envy me! I love you, little Hind, and I will take care of you and look after you.' And with this he went farther into the forest to find some green herbs for her.

Now the Hind with a sudden fright found its heels again, and, just because she wanted so much to stay, she bounded off as fast as she could go, and never stopped till she reached home, where in great excitement she told Giroflée all that had happened.

THE HIND OF THE WOOD

The Prince, when he returned and found that the Hind had disappeared, went back also to the hut, and told the old woman that the Hind had deserted him just when he had been so very kind to it and had gone in search of food for it. The Warrior Prince then explained to Becafigue that it was only to see the little Hind that he had remained so long, and that on the morrow he would depart and go away. But he did not.

The Princess in the meantime resolved to go a long way into the forest on the morrow, so as to miss the Prince; but he guessed her little trick, and so the next day he did the same as she. Then, suddenly, in the distance he saw the Hind so plainly that he let fly an arrow to attract its attention. What was his dismay to see the arrow pierce the flank of the poor little Hind! She fell down immediately on a mossy bank, and swiftly the Prince ran up. He was so upset at what had happened, that he flew and got leaves and stopped the bleeding. Then he said:

'Is it not your fault, little flier? You ran away and left me yesterday, and the same would have happened to-day if this had not occurred.'

The Hind did not reply at all; what could she say? And besides, she was in too much pain to do anything but moan.

The Prince caressed her again and again. 'What have I done to you?' he said. 'I love you, and I cannot bear to think I have wounded you.'

But her moaning went on. At last the Prince resolved to go to the hut and get something to carry her on, but before he went he tied her up with little ribbons, and they were tied in such a manner that the Princess could not undo them. As she was trying to free herself she saw Giroflée coming towards her, and made a sign to her to hasten; and, strange to say, Giroflée reached her exactly at the same moment as the Prince with Becafigue.

'I have wounded this little Hind, madam,' said the Prince, 'and she is mine.'

'Sir,' replied Giroflée, 'this little Hind is well known to me—

and, if you want to see how she recognises me, you will give her her liberty.'

The Prince then cut the ribbons in compliance with her request.

'Come along, my little Hind,' said Giroflée; 'kiss me!'

At this the little Hind threw herself on Giroflée's neck. 'Nestle to my heart! Now give me a sigh!' The Hind obeyed, and the Prince could not doubt that what Giroflée said was true.

'I give her to you,' said the Prince; 'for I see she loves you.'

Now when Becafigue saw Giroflée, he told the Prince that he had seen her in the castle with the Princess Désirée, and that he knew that Giroflée was staying in a part of their own hut. Why could they not find out if the Princess was staying there also? So the following night, the Prince having agreed, Becafigue listened through a chink in the wall of the hut, and what was his surprise to hear two voices talking! One said:

'Oh, that I might die at once! It would be better than to remain a Hind all the days of my life! What a fate! Only to be myself to you, and to all others a little White Hind! How terrible never to be able to talk to my Prince!'

Becafigue put his eye to the chink and this is what he saw.

There was the Princess in a beautiful dress all shining with gold. In her lovely hair were diamonds, but the tears in her eyes seemed to sparkle even more brightly. She was beautiful beyond words, and disconsolate beyond sorrow.

Becafigue nearly cried out with joy at sight of her. He ran off at once and told the Prince.

'Ah! seigneur,' said he, 'come with me at once and you will see in the flesh the maiden you love.'

The Prince ran with him, and when they came on tiptoe to the chink in the wall, he looked and saw his dear Princess.

Then so great was his joy that he could not be restrained. He went and knocked at the door, resolving to see his Princess at once.

Giroflée, thinking it was the old woman, opened the door, and the Prince immediately dashed into the room and threw himself at the feet of the Princess, and kissed her hand and told her how much he loved her.

'What! my dear little Princess, was it you that I wounded as a little Hind? What can I do to show my sorrow for so great a crime?'

The way in which he spoke put all the doubts from the Princess's mind. The Prince, knowing all, loved her. She bade him rise, and then stood with downcast eyes, fearing the worst. Her fears were justified: in a moment his arms were around her, and she was sobbing for joy on his breast.

They had stood a moment so, when suddenly the Prince started and listened. What sound was that? It was the tramp of armed men; nearer and nearer it came—the threatening sound of an advancing host. He opened the window, and, on looking out, saw a great army approaching. They were his own soldiers, going up against Désirée's father to avenge the insult offered to their Prince. And the King his father was at their head, in a litter of gold.

When the Warrior Prince saw that his father was there he ran out to him and threw his arms round his neck and kissed him.

'Where have you been, my son?' said the King. 'Your absence has caused me great sorrow!'

Then the Prince told him all about Long-Epine, and how the Princess had been changed into a Hind through her disregard of the Fairy's warning.

The King was terribly grieved at this news, and turned his eyes to heaven and clasped his hands. At this moment the Princess Désirée came out, mounted on a pure-white horse and looking more beautiful and lovely than she had ever been. Giroflée was also with her as her attendant. The spell had been removed for ever.

At sight of them the old King blessed them, and said that he would give his kingdom to his son as soon as he was married to the Princess Désirée. The Princess thanked him a thousand times for his goodness, and then the King ordered the army to return to the city, for there would be no war, but only rejoicing.

THE HIND OF THE WOOD

Back into the capital, a mighty procession—an army headed by its rulers, and victorious without striking a blow. Great was the joy of all the people to see the Prince and the Princess, and they showered upon them heaps of presents the like of which was never seen.

The faithful Becafigue begged the Prince to allow him to marry Giroflée. She was delighted to have such a great offer, and more than delighted to remain in a land where she would always be with her dear Princess.

Now the Fairy Tulip, when she heard all that had happened, resolved, out of the goodness of her heart, to give Giroflée a splendid present, so that her husband should not have the advantage of being the richer. It will astonish you to hear that she gave her four big gold mines in India; and you know what gold mines in India are worth.

And the marriage feasts lasted several months. Each day was a greater day than the one before; and every day the adventures of the little White Hind were sung throughout the country, even as they are still sung, in boudoir, fireside, and camp, to this very day.

IVAN AND THE CHESTNUT HORSE

A RUSSIAN FAIRY TALE

IN a far land where they pay people to keep its name a profound secret, there lived an old man who brought up his three sons just exactly in the way they should go. He taught them the three R's, and also showed them what books to read and how to read them. He was particularly careful about their education, for he had learned that to know things was to be able to do things.

At last, when he came to die, he gathered his three sons round his deathbed and cautioned them.

'Do not forget,' he said—'do not forget to come and read the prayers over my grave.'

'We will not forget, father,' they replied.

The two elder brothers were great big, strapping fellows, but the youngest one, Ivan, was a mere stripling. As they all stood around the bed of their dying father, he looked a mere reed compared to his proud, stout, elder brothers. But his eyes were full of fire and spirit, and the firm expression of his mouth showed great determination. And, when the father had breathed his last, and his two elder brothers wept without restraint, Ivan stood silent, his pale face set and his eyes full of the bright wonder of tears that would not melt.

On the day that they buried their father, Ivan returned to the grave in the evening to read prayers over it. He had done so, and was making his way homeward, when there was a great clatter of hoofs behind him; then, as he reached the village square, the horseman pulled up and dismounted quite near to him.

IVAN AND THE CHESTNUT HORSE

After blowing a loud blast on his silver trumpet—for he was the King's messenger—he cried in a loud voice:

'All and every man, woman and child, take notice, in the name of the King. It is the King's will that this proclamation be cried abroad in every town and village where his subjects dwell. The King's daughter, Princess Helena the Fair, has caused to be built for herself a shrine having twelve pillars and twelve rows of beams. And she sits there upon a high throne till the time when the bridegroom of her choice rides by. And this is how she shall know him: with one leap of his steed he reaches the height of the tower, and, in passing, his lips press those of the Princess as she bends from her throne. Wherefore the King has ordered this to be proclaimed throughout the length and breadth of the land, for if any deems himself able so to reach the lips of the Princess and win her, let him try. In the name of the King I have said it!'

The blood of the youth of the nation, wherever this proclamation was issued, took flame and leapt to touch the lips of Princess Helena the Fair. All wondered to whose lot this lucky fate would fall. Some said it would be to the most daring, others contended that it was a matter of the leaping powers of the steed, and yet others that it depended not only on the steed but on the daring skill of the rider also.

When the three brothers had listened to the words of the King's messenger they looked at one another; at least the elder two did, for it was apparent to them that Ivan, the youngest, was quite out of the competition, whereas they, two splendid handsome fellows, were distinctly in it.

'Brothers,' said Ivan at last, 'our first thought must be to fulfil our father's dying wish. But, if you prefer it, we could take it in turns to read the prayers over our father's grave. Let it be the duty of one of us each day to fulfil the duty, morning and evening.'

The elder brothers agreed readily to this, but, when Ivan asked whose turn it should be on the morrow, they both began to make excuses.

IVAN AND THE CHESTNUT HORSE

'As for me,' said the eldest, 'I must go and order the work of the farm my father left me, and that will take seven days.'

'And for me,' said the younger, 'I must see to the estate which is my part of the inheritance, and that also will take seven days.'

'Then,' replied Ivan, 'if I perform the duty for seven days, you will each do your share afterwards?'

His brothers agreed still more readily than before. Then they went their ways, Ivan full of thoughts of his father, and the other two to train their jumping horses, the one on his farm and the other on his estate. And both laughed to themselves, for neither knew the purpose of the other.

How they curled their hair and cleaned their teeth, and practised 'prunes and prisms' with their mouths close to the looking-glass!—so that when, at one bound of their magnificent steeds, they reached the level of the Princess's lips, to aim the kiss that was to win the prize, they would make a brave show, and a conquering one. As for their little brother, they each thought he could go on praying over their father's grave as long as he liked,—it would be the best thing he could do, and it would not interfere with their secret plans, so carefully concealed from each other and from him.

So, for seven days, in their separate districts, they raced about on their horses by day and dreamed of the greatest leaping feats by night. And at the end of the seven days the youngest brother summoned them to keep their agreement, and asked which of them would read the prayers, morning and evening, for the second seven days.

'I have done my part,' he said; 'now it is for you to arrange between you which one shall continue the sacred duty.'

The two elder brothers looked at each other and then at Ivan.

'As for me,' said one, 'I care little who does it, so long as I am free to get on with my business, which is more important.'

'And as for me,' said the other, 'I am in no mind to watch

each blade of grass growing on the grave. I cannot really afford the time, I am so busy. You, Ivan,—you are different: you are not a man of affairs; how could you spend your time better than reading prayers over our father's grave?'

'So be it,' replied Ivan. 'You get back to your work and I will attend to the sacred duty for another seven days.'

The two elder brothers went their separate ways, and for seven more days devoted their entire attention to training their horses for the flying leap at the Princess's lips. How they tore like mad about the fields! How they jumped the hedges and ditches! How they curled their hair and dyed their moustaches and practised their lips, not only to 'prunes and prisms,' but to 'peaches of passion' and 'pomegranates,' and 'peripatetic perambulation' and everything they could think of! In fact, they paid so much attention to the lips which were to meet those of the Princess at the top of the flying leap, that they began to neglect their own and their horses' meals. In other words, they were beginning to show signs of over-training.

At the end of the second seven days Ivan again summoned them to a family council, and asked them if either of them could now take up the sacred duty. But no; thinking heavily on horses and lips, and high jumps and kisses, they spoke lightly of fields to be tilled, seed to be sown, and all such things that must be done at once. Their view was—and they got quite friendly over it—that Ivan should be more than delighted to bear this pleasurable burden of reading prayers over his father's grave. Indeed, nothing but the stern call of immediate duty would prevail upon them to relinquish a task so pleasant.

'So be it,' said Ivan; 'I will perform the sacred duty for another seven days.' But as he spoke, he noted his brothers' curled hair and dyed moustaches, and gleaned from this, and from the look of sudden suspicion and jealousy exchanged between them, that they were both in love with the same fair one. But he kept this to himself, and left them to their own concerns.

Again, at the end of seven days, when Ivan had read the prayers devoutly, he summoned his brothers. But they did not come. Both sent messages saying that they were frightfully busy, and would he be so good as to go on with the sacred duty until they could be spared to do their share later on. Ivan accepted their messages, and went on reading the prayers over the father's grave.

Meanwhile each of his brothers prepared for the great flying leap; and each said to himself: 'What about Ivan? He would like to see this great exploit. It might make a man of him. He is altogether lacking in ambition, and to see a great deed done might stir him to try to be a great hero himself. But yet—I fear it would never do. He is so weedy, so insignificant. I feel I should lose by having a brother like that anywhere about. No; he is far better reading prayers over our father's grave.'

So each in his own way resolved to go in alone—apart from the other and apart from Ivan.

The morning of the great day came. The eldest brother had chosen from his horses a magnificent black one with arched neck and flowing mane and tail. The second brother had selected a bay equally splendid. And now, at sunrise, they were, each unknown to the other, combing their well-curled hair, re-dyeing their moustaches, and booting and trapping themselves for the wonderful display of prowess the day was to bring forth. And they did not forget to make sure that their lips were as fit as they were anxious for the 'high kiss.'

At the appointed time they rode into the lists and drew their lots, and neither was altogether surprised at seeing his brother among the host of competitors for the hand of Helena the Fair. Their surprise came later, when Ivan arrived on the scene.

It so happened in this way: that, towards evening, when his two brothers had each had their last try to leap up to the Princess's lips and failed, like every one else, Ivan himself was reading the prayers over his father's grave. Suddenly a great emotion came over him, and he stopped in his reading. He was filled with a longing to look just for once upon the face of Helena the Fair, for whose favour he knew that the most splendid in the land were competing with their wonderful steeds. So strong was this longing that he broke down and, bending over his father's grave, wept bitterly.

And then a strange thing happened. His father heard him in his coffin, and shook himself free from the damp earth, and came out and stood before him.

'Do not weep, Ivan, my son,' he said. And Ivan looked up and was terrified at the sight of him.

'Nay, my son, do not fear me,' his father went on. 'You have fulfilled my dying wish, and I will help you in your trouble. You wish to look upon the face of Helena the Fair, and so it shall be.'

With this he drew himself up, and his aspect was commanding. Then he called in a loud voice, and, as the echoes of his tones began to die away, Ivan heard them change into the far-distant beat of a horse's hoofs. After listening for a while his father called again, and this time the echo was a horse's neigh and galloping hoofs. It seemed beyond the hillside, and Ivan looked up and wondered. A third time his father called, and nearer and nearer came the galloping sound, until at last, with a thundering snort and a ringing neigh, a beautiful chestnut horse appeared, circled round them thrice, and then came to a halt before them, its two forefeet close together and its eyes, ears, and nostrils shooting flames of fire.

Then came a voice, and Ivan knew it was the voice of the chestnut horse with the proudly arched neck and flowing mane:

'What is your will? Command me and I obey!'

The father took Ivan by the hand and led him to the horse's head.

'Enter here at the right ear,' he said, 'and pass through, and make your way out at the left ear. By so doing you will be able to command the horse, and he will do whatever you may wish that a horse should do.'

So Ivan, nothing doubting, passed in at the right ear of the chestnut horse and came out at the left; and immediately there was a wonderful change in him. He was no longer a dreamy youth: he was at once a man of affairs, and the light of a high ambition shone in his eyes.

'Mount! Go, win the Princess Helena the Fair!' said his father, and immediately vanished.

With one spring Ivan was astride the chestnut horse, and, in another moment, they were speeding like lightning towards the shrine of Helena the Fair.

The sun was setting, and the two elder brothers, disconsolate, were about to withdraw from the field, when, startled by the cries of the people, they saw a steed come galloping on, well ridden, and at a terrific pace. They turned to look and they marked how Helena the Fair, disappointed of all others, leaned out to watch the oncoming horseman. And the whole concourse turned and stood to await the possible event.

On came the chestnut horse, his nostrils snorting fire, his hoofs shaking the earth. He neared the shrine, and, to a masterful rein, rose at a flying leap. The daring rider looked up and the Princess leaned down, but he could not reach her lips, ready as they were.

The whole field now stood at gaze as the chestnut horse with its rider circled round and came up again. And this time, with a splendid leap, the brave steed bore its rider aloft so that the fragrant breath of the Princess seemed to meet his nostrils, and yet his lips did not meet hers.

Again they circled round while all stood still and tense. Again the chestnut steed rose to the leap, and, this time, the lips of Ivan met those of the Princess in a long sweet kiss, for the chestnut horse seemed to linger in the air at the top of its leap while that kiss endured.

Then, while the Princess looked after, horse and rider reached the ground and disappeared like lightning.

Instantly the host of onlookers swarmed in.

'Who is he? Where is he?' was the cry on every hand. 'He

kissed her on the lips, and she kissed him. Look at her! Is it not true?'

It was true, for Princess Helena the Fair, with a lovelight in her eyes, was leaning down and searching, with all her soul, even for the very dust spurned from the heels of her lover's horse. But she could see nothing, and sank back within her shrine, treasuring the kiss upon her lips; while the people, dissatisfied, but wondering greatly, melted away. Among them went the splendid brothers, seeking how they could sell their well-trained horses to advantage, for they had both been frantically near to the Princess's lips.

Whither had Ivan flown on the chestnut horse? Loosing the reins—he cared for nothing but the kiss—he let his steed go, and presently it came to a standstill before his father's grave. There he dismounted and turned the horse adrift. As if its errand was completed, it galloped off; a rainbow came down to meet it, and, closing in, seemed to snatch it up in its folds. Ivan was alone before his father's grave.

Once more he bowed himself in prayer. Once more his father appeared before him.

'Thou hast done well, O my son,' he said. 'Thou hast fulfilled my dying wish, but my living wish is yet to be fulfilled. To-morrow Helena the Fair will summon the people and demand her bridegroom. Be thou there, but say nothing.'

With this Ivan found himself alone.

On the following day there was a great gathering at the palace, and, in the midst of it, sat Princess Helena the Fair demanding her bridegroom—the one who had leapt to her lips and won her from all others. Her heart and soul and body were his. The half of her kingdom to come was his. She, herself, was his;—where was he?

Search was made among the highest in the land, but, fearing a demand for the repetition of the leap and the kiss, none came forward. Ivan sat at the back, a humble spectator.

'She is thinking of that leap and that kiss,' said he to himself. 'When she sees me as I am, then let her judge.'

But love, though blind, has eyes. The Princess rose from her seat and swept a glance over the people. She saw the two handsome elder brothers and passed them by as so much dirt. Then, by the light of love, she descried, sitting in a corner, where the lights were low, the hero of the chestnut horse,—the one who had leapt high and reached her lips in the first sweet kiss of love.

She knew him at once, and, as all looked on in wonder, she made her way to that dim corner, took him by the hand without a word, and led him up, past the throne of honour, to an ante-chamber, where, with the joyous cries of the people ringing in their ears, their lips met a second time,—at the summit of a leap of joy.

At that moment the King entered, knowing all.

'What is this?' said he.

Then he smiled, for he understood his daughter, and knew that she had not only chosen her lover, but had won her choice.

'My son,' he added, without waiting for an answer, 'you and yours will reign after me. Look to it! Now let us go to supper.'

THE QUEEN OF THE MANY-COLOURED
BEDCHAMBER

AN IRISH FAIRY TALE

ONE day in the long ago, the sun shone down upon a green wood whose mightiest trees have since rotted at the bottom of the ocean, where the best masts find a grave. While the sunlight slept on the bosom of the foliage, a horseman galloped in the shade beneath. The great chief Fion, son of Cumhail, was looking for his knights, whom he had outstripped in the hunt.

He reined in his steed in a broad glade, and blew his bugle loud and clear. Beside the echoes repeated among the hillsides, there was no answering call. He rode on, pausing now and again to blow another and another bugle-blast, but always with the same result.

At length the wood grew more scattered, and presently he came out upon a stretch of plain where the grass was so green that it looked like emerald ; and beyond it in the distance, at the end of the sloping plain, he could see the seashore, and the ocean rising like a wall of sapphire up to the farthest horizon.

Down by the shore he could see figures moving, and, thinking that his knights had found their way thither, he rode like the wind down the long, gentle slope towards them. As he drew nearer and nearer, he saw that there were twelve of them, and they were playing at ball. By the mighty strokes they gave with the *coman**he guessed that these were the twelve sons of Bawr Sculloge, for none but them could drive the ball so high and far. Tremendous were their strokes, and, when they ran after the ball, they outstripped the wind.

As Fion drew rein and dismounted, they stopped their play ;

73

*Coman, bat

and, drawing near, welcomed him loudly as the helper of the weak, and the protector of the green island against the white-faced stranger.

When he had returned their greeting, they invited him to join them in their game—if such an amusement was agreeable to him.

'Fion, son of Cumhail,' said one, 'here, take my *coman* and wipe away the vanity and conceit of all comers, for we are practising for a great contest.'

Fion took the *coman* and looked at it, holding it up between his finger and thumb.

'I doubt if I could do much good with this plaything,' said Fion; 'it would break at first blow if I were to strike at all hard.'

'Never let that stand in the way,' returned the other. 'Wait!'

He then searched upon the ground among the blades of grass, and at length found a nettle, which he pulled up by the roots. Having breathed a charm over it, he passed it three times from one hand to the other, and lo, it was changed into a mighty *coman*, fit for the hand of Fion, son of Cumhail.

Then they were amazed at his terrific blows. The ball, struck by Fion, soared almost out of sight in the sky, and fell to earth far off. But, each time, the fleet-footed sons of Bawr Sculloge retrieved it.

At last Fion bared his arm to the shoulder, and, with a final blow, sent the ball out of sight. None saw it go; none saw it fall. They all stood and looked at each other.

'My hand on it,' said the eldest son of Bawr, advancing to Fion. 'I live to admit that I never saw the game played till to-day.'

As they were speaking, a voice hailed them; and, turning sea-wards, they saw a small boat approaching. As soon as it touched the beach, a man sprang ashore, and hastened towards them.

'Hail! Fion, son of Cumhail!' he cried. 'You are known to me, though not I to you. My lady, the Queen of Sciana Breaca, lays a knight's task upon you. Hasten forthwith, and have speech with her on her island. The hand of Flat Ear the Witch is upon her, and her chiefs have advised her to summon you to her aid.'

'I know it,' replied Fion. 'The Salmon of Wisdom, which comes up from the sea, breeds knowledge in my brain. I know what is passing in all the islands, but I fear that my efforts against witchcraft would be unavailing. Nevertheless, I will try. I will choose, from the twelve sons of Bawr Sculloge, three that I need, and together we will follow you to the island.'

'But, noble chief, you have no boat here, and mine will hold only one other beside myself.'

'Let not that trouble you,' replied Fion. 'I will provide a boat for us four, and we will follow you.'

With this he selected from the twelve sons the three that he needed. They were Chluas, Grunne, and Bechunach. Then he plucked two twigs of a witch hazel that grew near by, and they all proceeded to the beach. There he held the two twigs out over the water, and, in a moment, the one became a boat and the other a mast with sail set. He sprang in and the three followed, and presently they were speeding over the sea, setting their course by that of the stranger in his boat.

They sailed for many hours before they came to the island of the Queen of the Many-coloured Bedchamber. There they passed between high rocks, and entered a quiet harbour, where they moored their boat to a stout pillar and set a seal upon the fastening, forbidding any but themselves to loose it for the space of one year, for they knew not how long their quest would last. Then they went up into the palace of the Queen.

They were gladly welcomed and treated with the most generous hospitality. When they had eaten and drank, the Queen led them into a vast bedchamber decorated in the form and manner of the rainbow. Over the ceiling were the seven colours in their natural order. Round the walls they ranged themselves in the same fashion, and even the carpet itself was formed of seven hues to correspond. If the rainbow itself had been caught and tied up in a room, the effect could not have been more remarkable. It was indeed a many-coloured bedchamber!

QUEEN OF THE MANY-COLOURED BEDCHAMBER

Taking Fion by the hand, the Queen led them all into a corner of the bedchamber, where she pointed to a little cot in which a child lay sleeping.

'I had three children,' she said as she stood at the head of the cot, while Fion and the others gathered round. 'When the eldest was a year old it was carried off by that wicked witch, Flat Ear. The next year, when the second one was twelve months old, it suffered the same fate. And now my youngest here, who is twelve months old to-day, has fallen sick, and I fear to lose him in the same manner. This very night the witch will surely come and snatch my child away unless you can prevent her.'

'Take comfort, fair Queen,' said Fion. 'We will do our best. If you will leave this chamber to us we will watch over your child and see that it comes to no harm. And, if it be possible to capture the witch, depend upon it we shall do so. Too long she has worked her wickedness upon these lands.'

The Queen thanked him and withdrew. Soon the sun was set, and, as the child slept on and the shadows gathered, Fion and the three brothers set their watch in the Many-coloured Bedchamber. Presently servants came in and set wine before them—honey-mead and Danish beer, and metheglin* and sweet cakes. And, while they regaled themselves, the servants brought chessmen and a board, and Grunne and Bechunach played chess while Fion and Chluas watched by the bedside.

Hours passed while the two chess-players were absorbed in their game and the other two kept watch and ward. Then, towards midnight, while Fion was alert and wakeful, he saw Chluas sink his chin on his breast, overcome by an unnatural sleep. Thrice Chluas strove to rouse himself, but thrice he sank into a deeper sleep.

'Wake up, Chluas!' cried Grunne, as Bechunach was considering his next move. 'Wake up! We have a pledge to keep.'

Chluas roused himself. 'Yes, yes,' he said; 'we have a pledge

*Metheglin, type of mead liquor

to keep.' And then his chin sank gradually on his breast again, and he was once more a victim to the same unnatural sleep.

'Let him alone,' said Fion. 'I will watch.'

And the two brothers went on with their game of chess.

Suddenly a chill wind swept through the bedchamber. The fire in the grate flickered, and the candles burned low: the child in the cot stirred and moaned.

'See that!' said Fion in a hoarse whisper, pointing to the fireplace.

They turned and looked. It was a long, lean, bony hand reaching down the chimney and groping in the direction of the cot. The fingers were spread out and crooked, all ready to clutch. Slowly the long arm lengthened and drew near the cot. It was about to snatch the child, when Fion darted forward and seized it in an iron grip.

There was a violent struggle, for Fion had the arm of the witch in his powerful grasp. He held on so masterfully that the witch, in her frantic efforts to draw it away, fell down the chimney, rolled across the fire, struck Fion a terrific blow on the temple with her other hand, and then, falling on top of his unconscious body, lay still, her shoulder torn and bleeding.

Grunne and Bechunach quickly ran to Fion's aid, and, leaving the witch for dead, quickly withdrew his body and restored him to consciousness. Then, when they turned to see to the witch, they found that both she and the child had vanished.

They sprang to their feet and roused Chluas roughly. But he sank to sleep again immediately.

'What shall we do?' they all asked of Fion.

'Follow!' said he; 'follow where I lead. Grunne, pick up your bow and arrows; Bechunach, knot your ladder of cords. Follow me, both of you. Leave Chluas sleeping: he is not in his body; his spirit goes with us, and we cannot do without it.'

So Grunne gathered up his bow and arrows and Bechunach his rope, and the three, leaving the body of Chluas like dead wood, went forth to seek the witch.

QUEEN OF THE MANY-COLOURED BEDCHAMBER

They came to the seashore, loosed their boat, sped across the harbour and out between the high rocks. Then, guided by the loosed spirit of the sleeping Chluas, they sped forward on the ocean, driven by a freshening breeze. All the while the spirit-light, floating above the waves, led them on.

It was some two hours before dawn when they descried, in the distance, the lighted tower of the witch, upon an island. A dull, red flame shot out from it, and, as it turned for ever on itself, this flame lighted the sea around like a revolving wheel, clear and red against the surrounding blackness.

Nearer and nearer they approached it. Then Fion stood up in the boat and chanted magic spells, raising his arms and sinking them again with fingers stretched and his palms downwards. Then with a loud cry he called for sleep to descend on the vile witch of the revolving tower.

Ere yet his cry had died away on the surrounding sea the red light ceased to revolve. It was still, glaring dully. Then, as the boat touched the beach beneath the tower, Fion commanded Bechunach to throw his knotted cord and noose the topmost turret.

It was soon done. The noose caught, and held. And, in another moment, Bechunach, like a wild cat of the mountain, was climbing up. Fion and Grunne followed, while the spirit of Chluas, who lay fast asleep in the Many-coloured Bedchamber, guided and directed their every movement.

They gained a window of the tower and made their way in. Following the gleam of the dull, red light, they went from room to room, and at last came to one where it shone clearly through the cracks of the door. They burst in, and stood aghast on the threshold at the sight that met their gaze.

There on the floor lay the witch, in a magic sleep, the blood flowing from her shoulder, torn by Fion in the struggle. And there, around her, crying bitterly, were the Queen's three children.

Fion stooped down and swept his arm round them, and took

them aside and comforted them. Then he gathered the youngest to his breast, and, directing Grunne and Bechunach to see to the other two, he led the way to the window.

In a very short time they had all climbed down the rope ladder and were speeding away in the boat. But, as they left the island, the spell was released. The tower, with its wheel of red light, began again to revolve upon the waters, and they heard the witch's shriek of rage as she awoke to the pain of her wound, to find the children gone. It came again and again, that shriek of baffled hate and rage and pain. Then, as they looked back, they saw a dark form glide down the walls of the tower like a loathsome thing creeping head downwards. It reached the foot and sped to the seashore. Then it seemed to loose a boat, and, in another moment, it was speeding in pursuit of them. Faster and faster over the waves it came.

'Quick!' cried Fion to Grunne. 'Draw your bowstring to your ear. You will not miss: the spirit of the sleeper will guide your shaft.'

Grunne fitted an arrow to his bowstring, and drew it to his ear. Then, as Fion shot forward his outstretched hands, casting a vivid light from his finger-tips over the surface of the sea, the arrow sped with a twang and a whiz.

A terrible cry came back across the water. The witch, struck to the heart, threw up her arms, and, falling from her boat, sank in the sea.

Fion put down his hands, and then all was dark, save for a dull red light which flickered and played above the spot where the witch had sunk; and they sped on.

Now they neared the harbour, and saw a multitude of people waiting, with torches waving. When they gained the foothold of the land, with the three children in their arms, the people raised a mighty cheer. The Queen heard it and hastened to meet them.

Great was her joy on receiving her three children at the hands of Fion. And she showered upon him every blessing, entertaining him and his comrades—the three sons of Bawr Sculloge—for a whole year. And every year thereafter—lest the deed be forgotten—on the anniversary of the day she sent a boat laden with gold and silver and precious stones, and shields and helmets and chess-tables and rich cloaks; and the sons of Bawr Sculloge invited Fion to join them in high festival on that day, for they said, 'Such deeds should never be forgotten.'

And, one morning in spring, Fion, son of Cumhail, went into the gardens and orchards about his palace and plucked many twigs from flowers and fruit trees, and with these he went down to the seashore. Holding them above the waves, he recited a spell, and immediately a boat was formed of the twigs—a trim little craft with sail set.

He sprang in and steered his course for the isle of the Queen of the Many-coloured Bedchamber. And, as he sped over the waves, the boat began to bud; and green leaves appeared on the mast, and the spars and stays put out the growth of spring, till they shone like emerald in the sun.

When he came in sight of the island, the sides of the boat were covered with blossoms, the mast had put out a wealth of petals, and the sail and rigging were covered with flowering vines. Then, as he passed between the high rocks and entered the harbour, the watchers on shore saw a boat approaching, splendid with summer flowers, and on its mast were spreading branches dropping down with luscious fruit. Nearer and nearer it came, and, when it touched the shore, Fion sprang out, and bade them gather the beautiful flowers and the ripe fruit and take them to their Queen.

And Queen Breaca valued this present more than any other he could have offered, because the manner of it was beautiful, and a Queen is a woman, and a woman loves beautiful things above all else.

And Chluas, the sleeper—what reward had he? He claimed none, and none knows what was his reward. Yet it is said that in the Land of Deep Sleep there are rewards undreamt of by those who wake.

THE BLUE BIRD

A FRENCH FAIRY TALE

THERE was once upon a time a King who was tremendously rich both in money and lands. His wife, the Queen, died, and left him inconsolable. He shut himself up for eight days in a little room, and banged his head against the wall so much that it was believed he would kill himself, so grieved was he at his loss.

All his subjects resolved between themselves to go and see him, and they did. Some said that he could show his grief in a less painful manner. Others made speeches grave and serious, but not one of them made any impression on the widowed King. Eventually there was presented to him a woman dressed in the deepest mourning, and she cried and moaned so long and so loud that she caused no little surprise.

She said to the King that she did not like the others coming to ask him to stay his crying, for nothing was more just than that he should cry over the loss of a good wife; and that as for her, who once had the very best of husbands, and had lost him, she would cry for him as long as she had eyes in her head to cry with; and immediately she let out and redoubled her sobs, and the King, following her example, did the same.

Each one recounted to the other the good qualities of their dear dead ones; so much so that at last there was nothing more could be found to say about their losses and their great sorrow. In the end the widow lifted her deep veil, and the poor afflicted King gazed at the afflicted one, who kept turning and turning her great blue eyes with long black lashes. The King watched her with deep attention; and little by little he talked less of his lost Queen, until at last he forgot to talk of her at all.

THE BLUE BIRD

The widow then said that for ever she would cry and mourn for her husband, but the King begged her not to go to that limit and immortalise her sorrow. In the end he astonished her by saying that he would marry her, and that the black would be changed into green and pink, the colour of roses. It suffices to say that the King did as the stories tell : did all that was possible and all that she wished.

Now the King had but one daughter of his first marriage, and she was considered one of the eight wonders of the world ; her name was Florine, because she resembled a beautiful flower : she was fresh, young and lovely. She was always dressed in the most beautiful transparent clothes, and with garlands of flowers in her hair, which made a beautiful effect. She was only fifteen years old when the King married again.

The new Queen also had, by her first husband, a daughter, who had been brought up by her godmother, the fairy Soussio ; but she was neither beautiful nor gracious. The girl's name was Truitonne, because her face was so like the face of a trout, and her hair was so full of grease that it was impossible to touch it ; and her skin simply ran with oil. But the Queen did not love her any the less. All she could do was to talk of the charming Truitonne, and how Florine had all sorts of advantages over her ; and the Queen became desperate, and sought every possible way to make the King see faults in Florine.

One day the King said to the Queen that Florine and Truitonne were big enough to marry now, and that the first Prince who came to the court should have one of the two Princesses in marriage.

'I maintain,' said the Queen, 'that my daughter shall be the one to get the trousseau ; she is the elder, and she is a million times more amiable, and those are the points that matter, after all.'

The King, who hated disputes, said that it was well, and that she was her own mistress.

Some time afterwards, news came that Prince Charming had arrived. Never did a Prince display such gallantry and magnificence ; his manner and looks were in keeping with the name he bore.

When the Queen heard of this handsome Prince she employed all the dressmakers and tailors to dress Truitonne, and make her presentable, and she begged the King that Florine should have nothing at all new. Her one thought was to have all the beautiful clothes ready before the arrival of Prince Charming at court.

When he came the Queen received him in all pomp and splendour, and presented to him her daughter more brilliant than the sun, and more ugly than she was usually, because of all the jewels she had on.

Prince Charming turned away his eyes; the Queen tried to persuade him that the Princess pleased him very much. But he demanded to know if there was not another Princess called Florine? 'Yes,' said Truitonne, pointing with her finger; 'see, there she is, hidden away, because she is not good.'

Florine reddened, and looked so beautiful, *so* beautiful, that Prince Charming forgot himself. He bowed the knee and made a low curtsy to the Princess. 'Madam,' said he, 'your incomparable beauty is too much; but for you I should have sought help in a strange land.'

'Seigneur,' replied the Princess, 'I am sorry that I am not dressed in a proper manner, but I have only my old clothes; yet I thank you for asking to see me.'

'It would be impossible,' said Prince Charming, 'that any one once seeing you could have eyes for anything else than so beautiful a Princess.'

'Ah!' said the Queen, irritated, 'I do well wasting my time listening to you. Believe me, seigneur, Florine is also a coquette; she does not deserve that you should be so gallant to her.'

Prince Charming understood the motives of the Queen in speaking of Florine in this way. He was not in a position to prove the truth, but he let it be seen that all his admiration was for Florine.

The Queen and Truitonne were very upset to see that he preferred Princess Florine. So, when Princess Florine left the company of Prince Charming, the Queen with impatience waited for her to return to her room. There were hidden four men with masks over their faces, and they had orders to take the Princess Florine away on a journey, to await the pleasure of Prince Charming, so that she would please him better and would make him a better spouse.

The Queen then went to the Prince and told him that the Princess was a coquette, and had a bad temper; that she tormented the servants, and did not know how to behave herself; that she was avaricious, and preferred to be dressed like a little shepherdess rather than like a Princess.

To all this Prince Charming listened. 'But,' said he, 'it would be impossible for so beautiful and amiable a girl to be all that you say. How could that be true of one with such modest grace and beauty? even though she be dressed in a humble little frock. That is not a thing that touches me very much. It pains me far more to know that the Queen hurts her feelings, and you are not a step-mother for nothing; and really, madam, the Princess Truitonne is so ugly that it would be hard to find anything uglier amongst God's creatures. The courtiers, too, do not look at all pleased to hear you speak badly of Florine.'

The Queen spent half of the night questioning him, for she could not believe that he loved Florine. And the poor Princess Florine was terrified because the four men with masks had taken her far away.

'I do not doubt that it is for the Queen's advantage that I am taken away,' said she. And she cried so much that even her enemies were touched.

The Queen in the meantime gave Prince Charming all the jewels he could wish for, and lavished her attention on him. The King presented him with a little book with gold covers and studded with diamonds, and inside it, he told him, was a photograph of his future wife.

'What!' said Prince Charming, 'the beautiful Princess Florine? Ah! she thinks of me, and in a most generous manner.'

'Seigneur,' said the King, 'you mistake; we take the part of the amiable Truitonne. I am cross, seigneur, that you do not accept this great honour; but, at the same time, a King is merely a King: he is not master enough to make the engagements that he would like.'

The Prince at last asked for Princess Florine.

'Seigneur,' said the Queen, 'her father desired that she should go away until my daughter is married.'

'And for what reason,' said the Prince, 'should this beautiful girl be made a prisoner?'

'I ignore all that,' said the Queen.

So the Prince left the Queen's company because it was not congenial to him. When he entered his own room, he said to a young Prince who had accompanied him, and whom he loved very much, that he would give all the world to be able to speak to one of the women of the beautiful Princess for a moment. His young friend found one at once whom it would be possible to question with confidence. She told him that the same evening Florine would be at a little window that looked out on to the garden and that he could then speak to her, but that he must take every precaution, lest the Queen and King should overhear.

The Prince was delighted, and made ready to see the Princess. But the wicked maid went at once and told the Queen all that had passed. It was then arranged that Truitonne should take her place; and so, with great precautions, Truitonne placed herself at the little window.

The night was very dark; so much so that it was impossible for Prince Charming to suspect the change passed upon him. He expressed himself exactly the same to Truitonne as he had to Florine and plainly showed his love for her. Truitonne, profiting by her mother's instructions, said that she was the most unhappy person in the world to have such a wicked and cruel stepmother, and that she would have to suffer until her stepsister was married. The Prince assured her that he would marry her if she would have him, and that he would give her his heart and his crown; and he removed a ring from his finger and put it on the finger of Truitonne, as a token of his faith, and told her that she would only have to wait an hour, when a carriage would come to take her away. Truitonne begged of him to go to the Queen and ask her to give her her liberty, and assured him that, if he would come back to-morrow at the same hour, she would be ready.

The Queen was very happy at the success of her scheme. The Prince took a carriage drawn by three great frogs with great big wings, which made the carriage simply fly. Truitonne came out mysteriously by a little door, and the Prince, who was awaiting her appearance, at once put his arms around her and swore eternal faith, but, as he was not in any humour to take a long journey in the flying carriage without marrying the Princess whom he loved, he demanded of her where they could go. She told him that she had a fairy godmother named Soussio, who was a very celebrated person, and that they would have to go to her castle.

Then the Prince, not knowing the road, begged of the frogs with the flying wings to put them on the right way; and they did so, for, mind you, frogs know all the routes of the universe. And so, in no time, they found themselves at the castle of the fairy Soussio.

Then Truitonne told the godmother that she had trapped Prince Charming and that she wanted to marry him. The god-mother was not so sure that it could be done, 'for,' said she, 'he loves Princess Florine.' At all events she went to the room where the Prince was, and said to him: 'Prince Charming, here is the Princess Truitonne to whom you have given your faith; she is my godchild, and I wish that you marry her at once.'

'Me!' cried he; 'you want me to marry that little monster? You must think I am very easily pleased when you put forward such a proposition to me. She knows full well that I have never promised her anything. And if she says otherwise, she is——'

'Do not deny,' said the Fairy, 'and do not be bold and forget the respect that you owe me.'

THE BLUE BIRD

"The Prince took a carriage drawn by three great frogs
with great big wings...Truitonne came out mysteriously
by a little door."

Page 86

THE STORY OF BASHTCHELIK

"The Palace of the Dragon King."

Page 109

'I respect you,' replied the Prince, 'as much as it is possible to respect a fairy. Come, now. Will you deliver me my Princess?'

'Is it that you do not know me?' said Truitonne; and she showed him his ring, adding, 'and to whom did you give this ring at the little window as a pledge of your faith, if it was not to me? Come, now, do not pretend that you have forgotten.'

'No! no! I am not going to be duped and deceived,' said the Prince. 'Come! come, my great frogs! I want to depart at once.'

'You cannot depart without my consent,' said the Fairy, and she immediately touched his feet and they became glued to the floor.

'I will not,' said the Prince, 'have any other than my Princess Florine; on that I am resolved, and all you say and do will not change me one little bit.'

Soussio became sweet and used every art in her power to induce the Prince to marry Truitonne. Truitonne cried, raved, and begged; but the Prince would not say one single word to her; he only looked at her with indignant eyes and replied not a word to all her overtures.

He passed twenty days and twenty nights like this. At last the Fairy was so tired of it all that she said to the Prince, 'Very well; you are obstinate, and will not listen to reason, and will not keep your word and marry my godchild!'

The Prince, who had not spoken a word, at last replied: 'Do to me what you will, but deliver me from the dullness of this place!'

'Dullness!' cried Truitonne; 'bother you! You have done me a great injury in coming here to my country and giving me your word and then breaking it.'

'Listen to the touching words,' said the Prince in sarcasm. 'See what I have lost in refusing to take so beautiful a woman for my wife.'

'No! no!' replied Soussio, 'she shall never be that, and for your insult to her you shall fly through this window, and remain a Blue Bird for seven years. Do you hear me?—a Blue Bird for seven years.'

Immediately the Prince began to change, and his arms became covered with feathers, and he became a Blue Bird; his eyes became bright, and on his head a great white plume arose like a crown—and he flew away through the window.

In his sad mood he flew from branch to branch, warbling his song of sorrow and his love for Florine, and deploring the awful wickedness of their enemies. He thought that he was doomed for seven years, and that Florine would be married to another.

When Truitonne returned to the Queen and told her all that had happened she flew into a terrible temper. She resolved to punish the poor Florine for having engaged the love of Prince Charming. So she dressed the Princess Truitonne in all her grandeur, and on her finger was the ring given her by the Prince; and, when Florine saw this, she knew that the ring belonged to her Prince. The Queen then announced to all that her daughter was engaged to Prince Charming, and that he loved her to distraction. Florine did not doubt the truth of it all. When she realised that she would never marry her Prince Charming, she cried all the night, and sat at the little window nursing her regrets. And, when the day arrived for the marriage, she shut the window and continued to cry.

During this time the Blue Bird, or Prince Charming, did not cease to fly round the castle. The Princess sat at the window and every night entreated that she might be delivered. 'O wicked Queen!' she cried, 'to keep me shut up like this because of Prince Charming!'

The Blue Bird heard this and did not lose a word, but waited to see who the lady was who had such a sorry plaint. But she shut the window and retired. The Blue Bird, curious to see and to hear some more, came again the following night, and again there was a maiden at the window who was full of regrets.

'Fortune!' said she, 'you have taken from me the love of my

father. I have received a blow at a tender age; and it is so much pain that I am tired of living. I demand with all my heart that my fatal destiny may end.'

The Blue Bird listened, and then he knew that it was his Princess, and he said: 'Florine, a King who loves you will never love any one but you.'

'A King who loves me!' said she. 'Is this another snare of my enemies?'

'No, my Princess.' And Florine was very much afraid of this bird who spoke with as much spirit as a man. But the beauty of his plumage reassured her.

'Would it be possible to see you, my Princess?' said he. 'Could I taste a happiness so great without dying of joy? But, alas! this great joy would be troubled by your captivity, and the wicked fairy Soussio has done this for seven years.'

'And who are you, charming bird?' said the Princess caressingly.

'You have said my name rightly, and yet you fail to recognise me,' replied the Prince.

'What! The greatest King in the world! The Prince Charming!' cried the Princess. 'Is he the little bird I see?'

'Alas! dear Florine, it is too true! And, if one thing consoles me, it is that I prefer this sorrow rather than renounce the love I have for you.'

'For me!'

And so this went on. The Blue Bird paid visits to Florine every night, and they were as happy as it was possible to be. One evening Prince Charming flew away to his palace, and brought back lovely diamond bracelets, beautiful pearl necklaces and a sweet little pearl watch, and gave them all to Florine.

The Queen could not understand how it was that Florine had such lovely jewels and why she looked so happy, so she questioned her about it. Florine, who knew that if she said the Blue Bird had given them to her, they would not believe her, and would try to drive him away, said she did not know. The Queen said the Evil One must have bought her soul, and decided to watch.

She did so, and discovered that the Blue Bird came every night. Then Truitonne and her mother sought the help of the wicked fairy Soussio; and she, to please her godchild, worked another spell on the poor Blue Bird, so that he could not come any more to see his Florine.

One day his friend the Good Fairy was passing by a certain spot where he was a prisoner in a tree, and she saw a trail of blood and heard a very weak voice calling her, but nowhere could she find the Blue Bird. But she knew it was his blood. Then, after a long time, she found him in his tiny nest, dying.

This was the Good Fairy who had given him the flying-frog carriage, so again she resolved to help him if she could. Away she went to the fairy Soussio and asked her to release the spell on Prince Charming. Soussio agreed to do so if he would marry Truitonne. Then the Good Fairy conducted Prince Charming back to his castle, where, on his arrival, the ugly Truitonne was awaiting his return, dressed in lovely clothes, and more ugly than ever.

Now the old King died, and the people, who hated the Queen and her ugly daughter, said that they would have no other Queen but Florine, and they went to her in her little room and begged her for their sake to be their Queen. But she said she had not the heart for anything because she had lost her lover, Prince Charming. They asked her again to become their Queen and then to go out and look for him, and they were sure she would find him.

So she became their Queen, and then dressed herself as a poor peasant, and went out into strange lands and travelled in many strange places, thinking to find her beloved Prince. But it was all of no avail. One day she stopped, out of sheer fatigue, to rest by a fountain, and, while she was there, the Good Fairy, disguised, came by and asked her what she was crying for. Florine told her all about the Prince whom she loved and was seeking. Then the Good Fairy told her that Prince Charming was at his own castle and that the spell had been removed, and she gave Florine four little eggs, and said that whenever she was in trouble she was to throw one of them down, and at the same time ask what she wanted, and it would be granted. With these words she disappeared.

Florine turned her face towards the castle of the Prince, and, after many trials and sufferings, she found herself at the feet of her ugly sister Truitonne. Florine, disguised as a poor peasant, was not recognised, so she offered her lovely jewels for sale, and Truitonne, who loved jewellery, resolved to buy them. But Florine would not sell for money: all she asked was to spend a night in the castle. Truitonne was only too glad to get them at such a price, and agreed.

Feeling that the poor peasant girl was giving her something for nothing, and imagining that she did not really know the value of the jewels, Truitonne allowed her sister every liberty in the palace. She could go where she would, unquestioned, and do what she pleased.

Florine took every advantage of this, and, mixing freely among the attendants, she soon learned many things about Prince Charming. Among other pieces of news was this important item: the Prince, being unable to sleep, was in the habit of taking a sleeping-draught every night.

On hearing this she sought the Prince's head valet, and made herself so charming to him that he lost his head altogether, and was more than willing to fulfil her lightest wish.

'Tell me,' said she at last, 'why does the Prince take sleeping-draughts?'

'Ah!' replied he, looking very wise, 'it is because the Princess is so ugly.'

'Because she is so ugly? I—I don't understand.'

'What! From the very first the Prince's waking hours have been one long, frightful dream; and he can only banish it by night by taking the sleeping-draught. The Prince is deeply in love with the Princess's sister, but no one but myself knows that. Every night, when he sinks to sleep under the draught, he smiles, and his face looks so very happy, and he whispers one name again and again: "Florine! Florine!"'

The peasant girl's heart beat hard, and a plan shot like lightning through her mind. She would tell this man everything and he would help her. She knew he would, and she knew also that he would not be blind to his own advantage. Her mind was quickly made up. The four little eggs the Good Fairy had given her were packed in a little box. Taking this from the folds of her dress she took one of them and threw it on the floor.

'I *am* Florine!' she said. 'And I want your willing help.'

The head valet stared at her in dismay. Then his face changed. He bowed to her with the utmost respect, and said: 'Princess, I am your faithful slave; command me and I will obey.'

'First, then,' said Florine, 'do not give the Prince the draught to-night; and find me an apartment next to his.'

'It shall be done,' replied the valet, and with a low bow he withdrew to make the arrangement.

'Stay!' cried Florine as he was going. 'I forbid you to tell the Prince a word of this. You understand?'

'And obey,' he replied, bowing again and again as he left her presence, walking backwards in respect to high royalty.

That night the Prince, impatient to forget the face of Truitonne, called for his sleeping-draught. The head valet appeared, bearing a flavoured mixture in a crystal goblet on a golden tray. The Prince drank it. By its taste it was the draught, but, by its effect, it was not. No sleep came to him, and the face of Truitonne grew uglier and uglier in his mind. Presently he started up.

'What sound was that?'

It came from the next apartment—the sound of a woman weeping. He listened, and in the stillness of the palace the sound came clearly. He knew that voice: it was the voice of his dear Princess Florine, just as he used to hear it when, as a Blue Bird, he spoke with her at her window.

In a moment he arose and dressed himself in his royal robes.

While he was doing this, Florine in the next room took another egg from the box, and, throwing it upon the floor, cried: 'I wish that, by storm and lightning, all that is evil and ugly in this palace shall be destroyed, and all that is good and beautiful left.'

As she spoke the rising wind wailed about the palace and died away; dull thunder reverberated in the distance. The air grew stifling, and the night flowers paid their perfumes out like threatened debtors. Another rush of wind, then silence broken only by a peal of thunder nearer than before. The splash of heavy drops was heard on the flagstones of the courtyard below. The lightning was seen to flash through the windows, and the thunder shook the castle to its foundations.

Nearer and nearer loomed the storm, growing more terrific every moment. Every one was up and running about in panic. Those with ugly souls and bodies, if their consciences were also wicked, went mad in the panic, and fled in a body from the palace, thinking the end of the world had come. But those whose consciences were clear, whose hearts were true—those who could never be called ugly, no matter what they looked like—they sought the Prince and gathered round him, while the palace shuddered as all the storm gods poured out their wrath.

As the panic-stricken ones fled towards the hills, Florine looked out at the window and saw them, a rushing group with terror in their heels. There came a vivid flash of lightning, and the thunder split and rolled and crashed. When Florine looked again she saw no fugitives: they had disappeared for ever. Then, as suddenly as it had begun, the storm abated. The thunder rolled away into the distance, and the moon came out and rode from cloud to cloud triumphant.

There was a knock upon the door. It was the Prince, and behind him were gathered his own, the good and true, according to her wish. How could she meet him in her peasant's garb? A quick thought came to her. She took the third egg and smashed it on the floor, saying: 'I wish that I may come face to face with my Prince in all the dazzling splendour that befits a princess.'

Instantly there was a flash as if a fairy wand had cleft the air. And there stood Florine, the most splendidly royal figure you could imagine. She was beautiful beyond words—so beautiful that the wonderful jewels in her hair and on her lovely dress, on her neck and arms and tiny shoes, could never have got their beauty from any one but her.

She opened the door, and stepped back with a cry of delight. As she did so, she placed her hand to her breast where she felt the frail little box that contained the fourth and last egg.

In another moment she was in the Prince's arms, and the pressure of that embrace crushed the box and broke the egg.

'I wish,' she cried on the instant, raising her lips to his, 'I wish that you will love me for ever!'

BASHTCHELIK (OR, REAL STEEL)

A SERBIAN FAIRY TALE

THE aged Tsar was dying, and his three sons and three daughters were standing round his bed. He had yet strength to give his last commands, which were extraordinary.

'It is my will, O my sons,' he said, 'that you give my daughters in marriage to the first suitors that come to demand them. Question me not, but fulfil to the letter this, my last injunction. If you fail, my curse will fall upon you.'

These were the Tsar's last words before he died. It was approaching the hour of midnight when he passed away; and, when the dawn found his sons and daughters weeping for grief, they were startled by a dreadful noise. Came a loud beating against the palace gates, and instantly an awful tempest sprang up around the palace. Peal on peal of thunder roared, and vivid lightning flashed. The whole place rocked and swayed and trembled to its foundations. Then above the fearful din came a loud voice: 'In the name of a King, open the gates!'

'Do not open!' cried the eldest brother.

'See to it that you do not open!' insisted the younger one. But the youngest disregarded them both, and rushed to the gates.

''Tis I will open!' he flung back to them as they followed at his heels. 'Though the earth dissolve, what have we to fear? We have done no wrong!'

With this he flung the gates wide. There was no one there, but a sizzling light moved in towards them, and, out of the heart of it came a clear, cold voice:

'I have come to demand the hand of your eldest sister in

95

marriage. Forbid me not. I await your consent, but, if you refuse, it will be at your peril.'

The eldest brother answered at once, without a glance at the other two: 'It is unheard of! I cannot see you; I do not know you; who is to know where or how you will bestow my sister? I might never see her again.' He turned to the younger one and added, 'What say you, brother?'

'For my part, I will not consent,' replied he readily. 'I like not these signs of ill omen.'

Then they both turned to the youngest.

'What say you, little brother?'

He was quick to answer:

'I obey my father, and counsel you to do the same. It is not that I fear his curse, but I love him, and will obey his wish.'

Without waiting for any reply he ran within, and soon returned, leading his eldest sister by the hand.

'Here,' said he, 'offering her to the unseen visitant, 'in accordance with the custom of my country and the dying wish of my father, I give you my sister for your wedded wife. May she be faithful to you.'

The Princess was then taken by an invisible hand and led away; and, as she stepped across the threshold of the palace gates, a tremendous clap of thunder burst overhead; the lightning flashed again, and the whole earth rocked at the sound and sight of it; and, at terror of it, the courtiers who had gathered round fell on their faces and prayed for deliverance with all their might.

When the sun rose, the palace was still astir. None had slept, so none had dreamed; therefore, when eyes met eyes, the truth was known: a terrible thing had happened, but none knew how it had happened. All sought to find some clue to explain the disappearance of the eldest Princess, but there was no clue to the midnight mystery of the thing.

And on the second night the same terrible thing occurred again. The palace was stormed by thunder and lightning till its foundations quaked. Then, above all, came another commanding voice: 'Open the gates immediately—in the name of a King!'

Again the elder brother demurred, and again the youngest admitted the invisible but powerful applicant, and bestowed upon him the second sister.

'I trust she will be loyal and faithful to you,' he said; and, as she stepped over the threshold, the elements roared like a great lion glutting on his prey. And still, to the courtiers who stood by, the mystery of the thing was greater than their fear of the quakings of the earth and the sudden gasps of icy air that smote them.

Again, on the third night, while the youngest sister, who was very proud, was preparing to reject a suitor promised by her brothers, a greater storm than ever swept up about the palace, and, to hear it, one would have thought that half the world were rolling down a hill. It was terrific, and still more terrific was a voice that cried: 'Open these gates, in the name of a King who comes on his own business!'

As before, the two elder brothers demurred, but the youngest was more obedient to his father's dying wish. He bestowed the youngest sister upon the first to seek her hand. And, as she stepped over the threshold, the whole palace trembled and fluttered as if disturbed by the wings of a thousand giant eagles.

The two elder brothers mourned and grieved for their sisters, saying they were lost for ever. How could they see them again? How could they visit them? They were gone—swallowed up in the invisible.

'It is not so,' said the youngest. 'We have fulfilled our father's command. We have done no wrong; though the skies fall down, what have we to fear? Follow me forth: we will go and search for them!'

And so, not knowing what had befallen their sisters, nor whom they had married, they set out to search far and wide for them.

After journeying for some days, they reached a wild, inhospitable country, where, in a mighty forest so dense they could see neither the sun by day nor the stars by night, they lost their way. But still they pushed on, hoping to find an outlet. At last, after wandering for days, they came at sunset to a small lake, where they prepared to pass the night.

The eldest watched while the two younger brothers slept.

In the middle of the night, while his brothers slept soundly, he was gazing upon the waters of the lake, watching the moonbeams play with the ripples stirred by the soft night wind, when he saw a great black head appear on the surface and rapidly approach the shore where he was standing. Presently, as the monster emerged from the water, he found himself face to face with a great alligator rushing upon him to devour him.

Like lightning he drew his sword and smote the alligator between the eyes, cleaving its head in one mighty stroke. Then, when it had ceased its death struggles, he cut off both its ears and placed them in his haversack.*

As his brothers still slept he resolved to say nothing about the matter, and, to this end, he rolled the carcase of the alligator down the shelving shore into the water, where it sank like lead. At sunrise he roused his brothers, and, with few words, they resumed their wandering.

After three days struggling through the forest, they came to another lake, where they camped for the night. This time the second brother watched, while the eldest and the youngest slept.

And he, too, had a strange adventure, but more terrible than that the eldest brother had encountered. At midnight the waters of the lake began to move, and a great alligator with two heads emerged and came up on the shore. Then, with both mouths wide open and his long sharp teeth gleaming in the moonlight, the monster rushed at the watcher and the sleepers. But the watcher sprang forward, sword in hand, and dealt two terrific blows, one on each head, killing the alligator instantly. Then he cut off the four ears and placed them in his haversack, and rolled the huge carcase back into the lake. As the eldest brother had done, he kept the matter to himself, and let his brothers sleep on.

*Haversack, knapsack

BASHTCHELIK

In the morning he aroused them, and they all set out again on their wandering.

During that day they came to the edge of the forest, but only to find a vast desert before them. Their hearts sank within them, but, nothing daunted, they set forth, saying one to the other, 'There is no desert that has no boundaries. We shall come to the other side.'

But for three whole days they journeyed on, and all was still desert as far as the eye could see; and their food and water were exhausted, and they were sore distressed. Then, as they saw that the forest had no end, they cried to God to deliver them. And it seemed that the haze of the desert lifted, and they saw before them a lake, calm and peaceful. On its shore they would spend the night.

Having refreshed themselves from its waters, and eaten of some luscious fruits that grew upon its margin, they made their camp; and this time the youngest brother watched while the other two slept.

And he, also, had an adventure, but far more terrible than either of his brothers had encountered. As they were sleeping soundly, and he was looking at the still surface of the lake, something heaved up out of the depths and swam rapidly towards him. When it came up out of the water he saw that it was a monstrous alligator, with three heads. As it advanced upon him, with all three mouths wide open, ready to devour him and his sleeping brothers, he sprang to meet it, and, with three mighty strokes like flashes of lightning, severed the three heads from the body. Then he cut off the six ears and placed them in his haversack. As the other two brothers had done, he, also, kept the matter to himself.

It was not yet dawn, and the fire was burning low. In order to replenish it the young Prince went into the surrounding desert to look for fuel. After searching for some time in vain, he mounted a rock and looked around; and there, not very far away, he saw the gleam of a fire. He ran towards it, knowing he should find some fuel. But, when he arrived at the place where the fire was burning, he found the glare of it came from within a large cave. Creeping forward cautiously, he peered in, and saw a strange sight. The fire was blazing in the middle of the floor, and round it sat nine giants, gorging themselves on profane meats, whose flesh they drew from a huge cauldron over the fire.

Horrifying was this sight to the Prince. He made up his mind to trick the giants. He advanced boldly into the cave and gave them greeting.

'Good-morrow, my friends,' he cried jauntily; 'I've been searching for you everywhere.'

'Good-morrow, friend!' replied the biggest of the giants. 'And, if you're indeed one of us, you will, of course, join us in our feast, and then help us in our search for more.'

'With every pleasure!' cried the Prince; 'indeed, I need hardly thank you for the kind invitation, since I am at all times ready to assist you in your hunting expeditions. I have a rare tooth for the flesh of mortals, and the bigger they are the better I like them.'

The giants looked at one another and grunted approvingly. Then said the chief: 'Since you are with us, what is your name?'

'I am Nine Man Mord,' replied the Prince, taking the name of that hero of a far land who had slain nine men in so many strokes of his sword. 'I have journeyed from the North and have come to dwell among you, and be one of you.'

They were all astonished, for they had heard wonderful stories of Nine Man Mord; and they seemed to forget that they themselves were nine.

'Come, Nine Man Mord!' they cried; 'come, sit and eat with us.'

Readily the Prince took his place among them; but, though it seemed to them that he ate of the ungodly flesh, he did not really do so. While pretending to eat, he told them such tales of his adventures in the far country that none of them noticed he was not eating, but disposing of the flesh cunningly, sometimes by throwing it behind him, and again by offering a tit-bit to one or another in token of friendship.

When the feast was over, the giants rose and stretched themselves.

'Now,' said the biggest one, 'we'll go a-hunting. There's always to-morrow's feast to be thought of. We go, O Nine Man Mord, to the Tsar's city. There is still good flesh to be got there, though we have been feeding on it for many, many years. And, I may tell you, as the prey is not so plentiful as it used to be, it affords all the better sport in the taking.'

'I'm with you,' replied the Prince, 'and, maybe, I can show you a trick or two.'

So they set out and journeyed together—the nine giants and the Prince—till they came to the outskirts of a large and beautiful city. Here, in the surrounding forest, the giants plucked up two great trees by the roots, and took them to the city walls, where they placed one tree as a ladder.

Then the chief giant said to the Prince: 'O Nine Man Mord, climb by this to the top of the wall, and then we will pass the other tree up to you so that you can fix it as a ladder on the other side for all of us to descend by.'

The Prince climbed the tree-ladder; and, when he had reached the top of the wall they pushed the other tree up to him.

'Now,' he called down, 'I don't quite know how you want it placed. Will one of you come up and show me?'

In answer to this the chief himself climbed up and swung the tree over roots first, while he held and steadied it by its topmost branches. At this moment the Prince, unseen by the others, drew his sword, and, with one stroke, hewed off the giant's head. It fell within the city walls, and, in another second, the headless body went tumbling after it.

'Now,' he cried down to the others, 'it's all fixed, and your chief has gone down. Come up one by one, and I will hold the tree for you, and steady it, so that you can reach the ground quickly.'

And they came up one by one; and, one by one, off went their heads; and they, and their bodies after them, reached the ground very quickly. Then he climbed down the tree, and over the piled carcases of the nine giants, and made his way into the city.

BASHTCHELIK

It was true what the giants had said; for, although the sun had not yet risen, signs were not wanting that the city, if not deserted, was very thinly inhabited. The streets were neglected; the houses for the most part were falling to decay; and though, no doubt, those who remained—if any—feared a visit from the man-eating giants, still no watch was set, and the Prince, as he made his way through the streets, saw no one.

At last, as he went on, he espied a high tower, and, at one of its windows, there was a light. He made his way to this tower, and quickly ran up the stairs leading to the room that contained the light. At last, seeing its rays through the crack of the door, he turned the handle and entered.

A strange sight met his gaze as he stood a moment on the threshold. It was a splendid apartment of velvet and gold, magnificently decorated; but what immediately riveted his eyes was the figure of a beautiful princess sleeping upon a richly furnished couch. She was lovely to look upon; and, as he advanced into the room, he could see nothing but her. Presently, however, a hiss greeted his ears; and, looking up, he was startled to see a huge snake lying on the ledge above the couch, with its arched neck bent down ready to strike the sleeping girl.

With a loud cry the Prince tried to attract its attention; then, as it raised its head, he snatched his dagger from his belt, and, with one blow, pinned its head to the wall.

'Hold wood! Hold dagger!' he cried, releasing the hilt. 'None can draw that blade from the wall but him who planted it there!'

Then, without waking the beautiful maiden, he stole from the room and went back over the city wall, and beyond, till he came again to the giants' cave, where he quickly gathered some fuel and hurried back to his brothers, whom he found still sleeping. When he had set the fire in a blaze, he watched till the hour of sunrise, and then woke them with a loud cry:

'Arouse ye, my brothers; the day is here!'

But he told them nothing of his adventures of the night.

BASHTCHELIK

When they set out they came very soon to a high-road that led to the gates of the Tsar's city. Now it was the daily practice of the Tsar to walk in the ways of the city for an hour after sunrise, and bewail the death of those of his people who had perished by the hands of the giants, and also to pray fervently that his own daughter would never so perish. So it was that on this same morning he came, by his wanderings through empty streets, to the part of the wall where the tall tree-ladder was standing; and, as he drew near, he saw with amazement the great bodies of the giants lying on the ground, each with his head severed from his body.

When the Tsar saw this he raised his hands to high heaven and cried, 'This is a great day, for the giants are all slain!' And the people, who still remained to him, hearing his cry of joy, came running, and gathered about him, praying that God would preserve the mighty one who had done this astonishing deed. They were still praising the unknown hero, when some attendants came running swiftly from the palace, to tell the Tsar that a great snake had almost succeeded in killing the Princess.

At this he hastened back and made his way to the room in the tower where the Princess was lying asleep; and there he found the snake pinned to the wall by a dagger. At once he took the hilt in his hand and tried to drag it from the wall, but, to his great wonder, it resisted all his efforts.

On this, seeing the great strength of the hero who had planted the dagger there, and knowing that none but he could have the strength to remove it, he ordered a proclamation to be issued throughout the whole kingdom: that, if the man who had killed the nine giants and pinned the head of the snake to the wall with his dagger, would come and draw his dagger forth again, he would be rewarded with splendid gifts and receive the Princess in marriage.

Far and wide went this proclamation, but the Tsar, to make doubly sure, posted a thousand officials at as many inns on the great high-roads that connected the city with the outlying parts of the kingdom. And these officials' duty was to question travellers, and learn whether they had met, or heard of, any such hero as he who had killed the giants and transfixed the snake. Rewards were offered to any who could supply information, and punishments were held out to those who concealed it.

Now it so happened that the three Princes, in their search for their sisters, chanced to rest at an inn on one of the high-roads; and, when they had finished supper, they fell into conversation with an interesting stranger—a courtly man of cities, with manners that are only learnt in kings' palaces. He begged to be allowed to call for wine,—which in those days was no offence,—and, as they drank their toasts, he fell to narrating his wonderful exploits in a far-off kingdom—so far-off, indeed, that imagination alone could reach it, and no other traveller could ever return to tell a different tale.

After describing some heroic combats the stranger at last remarked, 'And what may be the doughty deeds that you young heroes have set to your credit?'

At this the eldest brother told how he had slain the alligator; and, to vouch for the truth of his story, showed the two ears he had preserved, placing them before the stranger.

When the unknown had applauded his story the younger brother told how he had slain the alligator with *two* heads, and threw down on the table the four ears as evidence.

The stranger applauded more loudly than before, and then turned to the youngest brother; but he remained silent.

'Come,' said the stranger, coaxing him; 'your brothers have performed great exploits: have you not followed their example?'

Then the young Prince replied: 'I am only young; but, now I think of it, I *did* kill an alligator once, myself. It was a rather ferocious beast in its way, and had *three* heads; but I managed to— well, here are its ears.' And he threw the six ears on the table.

At this his two brothers were as much astonished as the stranger; for, though he was the youngest, he had done the bravest deed. The official—for such was the stranger—then begged the young Prince to tell of his other exploits. So the hero told how he had slain the giants. This was enough for the official: he sprang up and hastened away to the palace, where he informed the Tsar that he had found the mighty hero for whom every one was searching.

The Tsar was delighted; and having rewarded the official, sent for the Princes in all haste. When they arrived, he bade them tell all they had been through, and listened to their adventures with all attention. And, when they had finished, he turned to the youngest brother and said: 'Your exploits, young sir, are the most extraordinary of all I have heard. But all of you follow me to the tower; I would make certain—*quite* certain!'

Beckoning the three brothers to follow him, he led the way; and, finally, they reached the room where the youngest had pinned the snake's head to the wall.

The couch was empty, but the snake and the dagger were still there, just as the young Prince had left them.

Then said the Tsar, addressing the eldest: 'Draw forth the dagger!'

The eldest brother seized the hilt, and put forth all his strength; but the dagger did not move.

Then said the Tsar: 'It is so. Let your younger brother try.'

His words were obeyed; but the dagger was immovable.

Then said the Tsar: 'It is so. Let the youngest try.'

His words were obeyed. The youngest Prince took the hilt, and, with a mighty wrench, tore it from the wall; then, as he restored it to its sheath at his side, the snake fell at his feet.

'It is so!' said the Tsar. 'It was your hand saved my daughter's life. I will give her to you in marriage, and you shall be my Prime Minister.' Then, to the two elder Princes, he said: 'If you would prefer to remain with your brother in my country I will bestow two ladies of the land upon you for wives, and give you suitable castles to live in.'

But, though the youngest accepted the Tsar's offer with a proud pleasure, the other two excused themselves with thanks, saying that it was only right for their brother to remain, but, for themselves, their duty was to carry out the quest for their lost sisters.

The Tsar honoured their refusal, and, having given orders that they should be escorted from the city with every mark of royal favour, bade them farewell; and they departed the richer by two asses laden with gifts of gold and silver and precious stones. Shortly afterwards, the youngest Prince and the Princess were married; and the whole city rejoiced for three days with great celebrations.

But the Prince, much as he loved his wife, soon began to blame himself for accepting this great happiness so easily when the quest of his lost sisters was his first duty. On this account he began to pine, and the Princess could not comfort him.

One day, when his grief threatened to sink him in remorse, the Tsar came to him with a bunch of nine keys in his hand, and said: 'My son; I am going forth to the hunt; but you remain, and, with these keys, you may open some delights while I am absent.'

Then he took him and showed him the doors of nine rooms of the palace, assuring him he would find great joy in the first four, a more hidden joy in the next three, and, in the eighth, a summing up of all the joys in the four and the three; but—the ninth he must not enter; for, what was there, no man could endure.

When the Tsar had gone to the hunt, the young Prince opened the doors one by one, and he was truly amazed at what was revealed to him. The first four led him to all the delights of earth; the next three to all the delights of heaven; and the eighth to the Great Joy of Earth and Heaven in one.

And now he stood at the door of the ninth.

'What is here?' said he. 'What is here that is denied me? I have slain the three-headed alligator; I have hewed off the heads of nine giants; I have vanquished the serpent that encircles the world, and rescued the Princess from his lowering fangs. Surely the Tsar is testing me! Come what may, I will enter at this door; for he who does not go on, slides back.'

BASHTCHELIK

With this he selected the key; and, inserting it in the lock, opened the ninth door, and entered. What an unexpected sight was there! The joys of the four, the three, and the eighth—were they at last bound up in this?—this man with the strength of the under-world in his limbs, the strength of the mid-world in his set face, and the strength of the skies in his calm gaze beneath tortured brows?

There, before him, was a man, bound, it seemed, by all the bonds of the universe. His legs were encircled with bands of iron, which, at their fastenings into the floor, were rusted. His hips and loins were bound with lead. A copper girdle held his breast. A silver band enthralled his tongue and hands, and what seemed like a spider's web of thin, light-blue wire encircled his body and gathered itself in a circlet of the same woven material upon his brows. Truly, if ever a man was fast bound, this man was; for, in addition to all these things, there was a ring of gold round his neck, and from it extended thick cables of platinum, which were firmly riveted into four strong beams, one in each corner of the room. Around him, on the eight sides of the room, were open windows revealing all the joys of the eight chambers; but the man was bound in the centre.

And, as the Prince looked upon him, the captive gasped, 'O young man, for the love of God, bring me a cup of water from yonder fountain; and I, in return, will give thee another life.'

The Prince at once drew him the draught from the nearest fountain, thinking the while that it would be good to have a life to spare. Then, when the chained captive had drunk the water eagerly, the two looked at one another.

'What is your name?' asked the Prince.

'My name is Bashtchelik, which, as you know, means "real steel."'

'Farewell, then, Bashtchelik; I hear the hoof-beats of the Tsar's horses in the distance.' And he turned towards the door.

'Nay, leave me not!' cried Bashtchelik, and then he implored him: 'Give me a second cup of water, and I will give you a second life.'

BASHTCHELIK

The Prince drew him another cup of water and handed it to him with a good heart, thinking, as it was returned to him empty, that a second life was well worth having. Then, hearing the approach of the Tsar more distinctly, he bade farewell a second time and turned away; but the captive again besought him.

'O mighty one!' he cried; 'do not leave me. I know thee, I know thy name; I know thy noble deeds. Twice hast thou given me to drink; I pray thee, do it yet a third time and I will give thee a third life.'

Hastily the Prince filled the cup and gave him to drink, for the Tsar and his company were now at the gates, and he knew not how to face him. But, before he could gain the door, he heard a crash behind him; and, looking back, he saw that the captive had broken his bonds and stood free. Then, before one could say it had happened, he had loosed a great pair of wings from his sides, and rushed through the doorway. The Prince, looking out, saw him snatch up the Princess, his wife, from the terrace of the Palace, and soar rapidly away.

Ere the beating of wings was lost in the distance, the Tsar came in and demanded to know why the ninth room was open and the captive gone. The Prince then explained everything, and begged the Tsar not to be angry.

'He broke his bonds,' he said, 'and has gone, taking my wife—the daughter that you gave me—away with him. But give me leave, and I will find her and kill Bashtchelik.'

'Alas!' replied the Tsar, 'you have done a rash thing. You know not this man. I lost the best part of a whole army in capturing him. What can you do, my son?'

'I will go forth and seek him,' replied the Prince without wavering. 'If he is stronger than I, then you will see neither me nor my wife again; but, if I prevail, we will return to you.'

So the Prince set forth on his quest; and after three days journey, he came to a beautiful city. And, as he rode beneath the walls of a castle, he heard a voice from a window high in the tower, calling to him. He drew rein and dismounted; then, as he advanced into the courtyard, a girl came running towards him.

'O my brother!' she cried; 'you have come at last!'

It was his eldest sister whom he had found so easily. They embraced and kissed, and then she led him into the castle.

'And your husband?' he asked as they stepped aside into a dimly-lighted antechamber; 'who and what is he?'

'He is the Dragon King,' she replied in a whisper; 'and he is no friend of my brothers. Yet I will hide you, and then ask him what he would do if you sought me out.'

That evening, when the Dragon King came home on whirring wings, there was no sign of either the Prince or his charger. Yet he raised his nostrils in the air and sniffed.

'I smell a human being,' he said. 'Confess, woman; who is it?'

'No one,' replied she. But he was certain about the matter, saying that his senses had never yet deceived him, though a woman might.

'That is nought,' said she. 'But, tell me; if my brothers came to look for me, how would you take it?'

'If your eldest brother came here,' replied the Dragon King, 'I would eat him raw. Your second brother I would stew gently over a slow fire, or, if he were nice and fat, I should roast him to a turn; but your youngest brother—him I would spare.'

Then said she, 'O King, my youngest brother, who is your brother-in-law, is here in your castle. I will summon him.'

It was a great meeting between the young Prince and the Dragon King. One would have thought that they had known each other for years. They embraced and wished each other health and long life; and then they sat down to a sumptuous banquet quickly brought in by winged attendants, who were evidently of the un-educated dragon classes;—indeed, though richly attired, they looked like slaves.

BASHTCHELIK

In the course of conversation the Prince happened to mention that he was on the track of one Bashtchelik, who had run off with his wife against her will.

'Bashtchelik!' exclaimed the Dragon King. 'My dear brother, I beseech you, seek him not. This kingdom itself put out five thousand strong, and took him unawares. But he escaped by a trick, gave battle to ten thousand of my picked dragons, fought his retreat to the mountains, and so escaped triumphant. Man to man—you against Bashtchelik—you cannot hope to win. If you will go back to your home, I will give you an escort and three asses laden with gold.'

'Three asses laden with gold!' said the Prince. 'I thank you much, but I have better than that: I have three lives, which I won from Bashtchelik himself. I will seek him and reclaim my wife.'

The Dragon King wondered at his words; then, plucking a feather from his wing, he said, 'You are determined, and I wish you well. Take this feather, and, if at any time you want my aid, burn it and I will come to you instantly with ten thousand chosen dragons.'

The Prince thanked him, and placed the feather in his girdle. The next morning he took leave of his sister and the Dragon King, and set out in search of Bashtchelik.

He left the city and crossed a desert, where he endured fatigues and encountered perils; but still, by his strong right arm, he preserved his three lives. Then, at last, he came to a city; and, as he took the mainway of it, the same thing happened as before. It was a woman's voice calling from a castle tower: 'O Prince! Dismount and come in hither!'

Again he made his way into a courtyard, and again he was met by a woman—his second sister—who greeted him with joy. Soon she led him into her boudoir, and immediately he asked: 'My sister, who is your husband?'

'He is the Eagle King,' said she.

Then, as it had happened with the Dragon King, so it happened with the Eagle King. He came whirring home from a great height, and, by the artfulness of his wife, he met and embraced the young Prince; for, though the Eagle King would have pecked out the livers of the elder brothers, he was glad to meet the youngest. A feast was spread, and, afterwards, the talk led on to Bashtchelik.

'Bashtchelik!' cried the Eagle King. 'Young man, will you listen to me? Once we battered him with ten thousand pairs of wings and assailed him with ten thousand beaks, but he triumphed. For one man to go up against him is as a thistledown attacking a whirlwind. Do nought. Stay with me: I will give you all you desire.'

But, as the Prince held fast to his purpose, the Eagle King plucked a feather from his wing and gave it him.

'If you are in sore straits,' he said, 'burn this feather, and, on the instant, I will come to your aid with ten thousand eagles.'

Then the Prince, thanking the Eagle King, set forth once more. And, in his further journeying, he again came to a city, and heard, beneath a castle wall, a woman's voice calling to him.

It was his youngest sister. She also contrived to bring him face to face with her husband, the Falcon King, who warned him strongly against Bashtchelik, and gave him a feather from his wing in case of need.

After a long search and many adventures, the Prince at last found his wife, standing at the mouth of a large cave. She was much surprised to see him, and ran forward to embrace him. He then told her all he had done since their parting, and she clung to him in great joy.

'Now, dear wife,' he said at last; 'now that I have found you, we will go together to your father's palace.'

'But Bashtchelik!' she exclaimed.

'Bashtchelik is not your husband,' he replied; 'I am your husband.'

'Yes, yes; but if we flee, beloved, Bashtchelik will surely follow us. His rage would be terrible, and I should lose you for ever, and find a frightful punishment.'

'Nay, nay; I am your husband, and I will protect you; come! Then he added to himself, 'She does not know I have three lives now, and I doubt whether Bashtchelik could kill me three times.'

So they fled together. But, some hours later, Bashtchelik returned from hunting and found the Princess had gone. From some footprints outside the cave he gleaned that she had not gone alone, and instantly guessed that her husband had carried her off. With a cry of rage he sprang into the air, and began to fly round the cave at terrific speed, and in ever-widening circles.

The sun was low down on the Western horizon when the Prince, riding hard with his wife on the saddle-bow, heard a whirring sound in the sky and looked up.

'Hasten!' cried the Princess in alarm; 'it is Bashtchelik. If we can reach the shelter of yonder forest he may not see us.'

But hardly had she spoken when an angry cry from afar fell on their ears. Bashtchelik had seen them—seen her long, yellow hair floating on the breeze and gleaming like gold in the rays of the setting sun. He swerved and swooped downwards, and, madly as they rode for the edge of the forest, he was upon them by the time they reached the outskirts.

Alighting on the ground, he tore the Princess from the Prince's arms, and cried out in sorrowful anger, 'O Prince, I gave you three lives out of gratitude to you, but, if you attempt to steal your wife again, I will kill you.' And with this he mounted in the air with the Princess, and soon disappeared in the distance, leaving the Prince lost in wonder at the suddenness of it all.

Nevertheless he was not to be beaten. He returned to the cave under cover of night, and, having concealed his steed, crept forward and hid himself near the cave, to wait until Bashtchelik should go forth to the hunt.

And he was not disappointed. Soon after the sun rose, Bashtchelik came out from the cave, bearing his bow and arrows, and went in search of prey. Then, when he was out of sight, the Prince dashed into the cave, took his wife and rode away with her. But again ere sunset they heard the whir of wings; and again Bashtchelik snatched the Princess from the Prince's arms. And this time he placed an arrow on his bowstring and drew it to the full.

'O Prince,' he said, 'I give you your choice: will you die by arrow or sabre?'

'By sabre,' said the Prince, feeling for his own.

'Nay, nay!' returned Bashtchelik, relenting. 'Because I gave you three lives, I pardon you a second time; but, if you attempt to steal your wife again, I shall slay you without a thought.'

But the Prince, as he watched Bashtchelik fly away with his wife, was not daunted. 'I wish he would stay to fight,' said he; 'but maybe he will next time, for I shall certainly take her again.'

And he did. And again they were overtaken. On this occasion it was nowise different, save that when Bashtchelik forgave the Prince it was in angry and threatening tones, before bearing the Princess away.

Having failed three times, the Prince rode sadly homewards. But he had not gone far when he bethought him of the three feathers given him by his brothers-in-law, and of their promises of help. He reined in his steed, and turned and galloped back. He would beard Bashtchelik in his cave, and then give battle, with three armies at his call, if, perchance, this powerful foe should seem to prevail.

When he reached the cave it was an hour after sunrise. He leapt from his steed and entered without knocking. There was a fire burning within, and his wife sat by it with her head on her hand, thinking. She sprang up at the sound of his footstep.

'You!' she cried. 'Ah! my beloved, you are in unseemly haste to quit this life, since you come for me a fourth time.'

'Listen to me,' he said; 'for you are my wife, and none shall keep you from me.' Then he showed her the three feathers, and explained to her that they were pledges of help in time of need. He placed them in her hand, and gave her also the burning-glass he used for kindling a fire, and said: 'Do not burn them until you see the combat is going against me. He will certainly follow us, but, this time, I think he will fight.'

The Princess seemed to agree to his wish, and, soon afterwards, they set out and rode rapidly away.

It was high noon when they heard the whir of wings and knew they were followed. Bashtchelik approached at a great speed, and they saw his sabre flashing in the sun. The Prince drew rein and dismounted; then, drawing his weapon, he advanced to meet his foe. But, ere their sabres clashed, the Princess, fearful for her husband's life, had taken the burning-glass and pinned the sun's rays to the feathers. A tiny curl of blue smoke arose, and then they burst into flame.

Instantly—ere yet the heart could beat twice—there was a shrill chord of three sounds, and as many colours shimmered like lightning in the air. Then as the feathers blazed, came dragon hosts upon the plain; flaming eagles flocked in; and the Falcon King with his myriads swooped down. Bashtchelik was surrounded on three sides, but he dealt a mighty stroke at the Prince's heart; and then, seeming invincible, fought his way through with much slaughter and gained the side of the Princess. Before she knew it she was caught up, and Bashtchelik was bearing her on rapid wings away.

But the Prince? Among the thick of the slain the three kings —his brothers-in-law—found him dead! But they took thought together as to how they might recall him to life, and at last decided to send for some water from the Jordan. They summoned three of the swiftest dragons and asked how long it would take to fetch it. 'Half an hour!' said the first. 'Ten minutes!' said the second; but the third said at once, 'Nine seconds!'

So they dispatched him; and, like a flash, he winged his fiery flight, returning in nine seconds with the water from the Jordan. With this they bathed the Prince's wounds, and they healed up at once; and lo, he rose up alive and well, but with only two lives left to him.

'Venture not again,' was the counsel of the three kings. 'Go not forth against Bashtchelik, for he is perfect steel, the mightiest of all; and none can conquer him: he has all Force behind him.'

But the Prince would not accept their words of warning. 'Force is not the strongest thing,' he said. 'Force is hard as steel, yet it can be overcome by the will of Love, which is so soft that it melts at a touch. In that I go forth again to conquer Bashtchelik, and regain my wife.'

They could not restrain him, but, ere he went, they counselled him again: 'Since you are willing to risk all, you must go; but think not that by mighty blows you can conquer Bashtchelik. Get speech with your wife, and bid her learn from him, by a woman's wit, wherein the secret of his strength lies. Then come and tell us; and, with that knowledge, we can help you to slay him.'

The Prince agreed, and parted from them. Making his way very cautiously to the cave, he waited till Bashtchelik had gone forth to the hunt, and then entered and found his wife, and bade her glean from Bashtchelik the secret of his strength. Then he returned to his place of concealment.

That evening, when Bashtchelik returned to the cave, the Princess praised his great strength and flattered him mightily upon it.

'Tell me, I pray thee,' she said at last, 'wherein thy great strength lieth, and wherewith thou mightest be bound; for'—with a laugh—'I would fain bind thee with my hair.'

Bashtchelik laughed, well pleased at her words. 'Wouldst thou know it?' said he. 'My strength is in my sword; were that taken from me I should then be weak, and be as another man.'

The Princess then bowed down before his sword and did homage to it, and sang a great song of joy that all power on earth was in the sword. But, on hearing this, Bashtchelik laughed, and laughed again, saying, 'Foolish one! my real strength lies no more in my sword than in its scabbard.'

'Then,' said she, 'thou hast mocked me. Tell me, I pray thee, wherein thy strength lieth.'

'In my bow and arrows,' replied he. And at once the Princess bowed down and did homage to his bow and arrows, singing their praise: how swift their flight through the air, how true their aim, how deadly their piercing points.

But Bashtchelik laughed again, and again, and again.

'Foolish one!' said he. 'My real strength lies not in my bow, nor in my arrows. But, tell me, why do you seek to know the secret of my strength?'

'Because I am a woman; and was there ever a woman who loved a man and did not want to know his secret?'

'Ay—to know it, and to impart it to others.'

'Nay, nay; to know it is enough. Tell me, I pray thee, and tell me truly, wherein the secret of thy great strength lieth.'

At this he was much distressed, and, thinking that the Princess believed her husband dead, he hoped at last to win her love; and so he told her.

'Listen to me,' said he. 'Far away in a high tableland in the interior of this country there is a mountain reaching up to the sky, and rooted far down into the earth. In a spot of that mountain—in a den where a serpent lies asleep—there is a fox, and in its heart there hides a bird. That bird is the storehouse of my strength. One flutter of its wings would scatter a whole army; one beat of its heart would shake the whole world—if the fox so willed it. But the will of the fox is over mine, and what strength I have comes from the bird through the will of the fox. And that fox is the hardest thing in the world to catch: it can take any shape it likes. So, now, you know all.'

'You have told me truly?'

'I do not laugh: I have told you truly.'

Then the Princess dallied with him, giving ear to his tales of terror and triumph. But, when he had supped and fallen asleep, she stole out and told the Prince all about it. And he, bidding his wife farewell, rode off in haste to tell his brothers-in-law. When they heard his news they called up their forces—the dragons, the eagles, the falcons—and proceeded forthwith against the mountain on the high tableland.

By certain signs the Prince discovered the den of the sleeping serpent, and there they surprised the fox, who, seeing the vast array on the sides of the mountain and on the plain, quickly took refuge in flight. But a host of eagles and falcons tore after him and overtook him near a great lake. Here he changed himself into a duck with six wings, and dived and disappeared. Presently, far away on the lake, they saw him reappear on the surface, and rise from the water, and wing his way up into the clouds. Immediately the dragons gave chase, and the eagles and falcons strove to encircle the swift-winged bird. Finally, seeing no way of escape, the duck swooped to earth, and changed again into a fox. Then the pursuers pounced and caught him.

The three kings then consulted together and decided to cut open the fox and take its heart out. This was soon done; then they built a great fire and threw the heart into it. And, as it burned, they saw a bird fly from it through the flames and fall scorched at their feet. Now, as they gazed upon it, it changed rapidly, growing in size and altering in shape, until at last there lay before them the body of Bashtchelik, his wings all burnt and his body charred.

So this monster perished, and the Prince regained his long-lost bride.

THE FRIAR AND THE BOY

"The Friar, bound fast to the post, squirmed and wriggled,
showing plainly that he would foot it if he could."

Page 126

THE GREEN SERPENT

"Laideronnette kissed and embraced the good
Fairy Protectress."
Page 141

THE FRIAR AND THE BOY

AN ENGLISH FAIRY TALE

'You good-for-nothing boy, you! It's always meal-times when you come home: that's all you care about here. Look at the knees of your trousers; why, playing marbles in the street with all the other filthy little brats is about all you're fit for. How d' you think I'm going to spend all my time patching up your holes and tatters? Drat you! Get out of it and wipe your boots before you come into a clean kitchen. I've been all the afternoon tidying up for the good Friar's visit this evening, and now you——'

'Hang the good Friar!' said Jack under his breath, for he was sick and tired of his stepmother's sour tongue, and more than sick and tired of the good Friar, who, he knew, was only 'good' when he was not feeling well. Taking a fairy-tale book from the shelf he went and sat in the inglenook, thus sheltering himself from a further storm of abuse from his stepmother.

The fact of the matter was, that thrice upon a time his father had married. Jack, a merry-hearted boy, and lovable for all his mischief, was his son by his first wife. The other two had no children, and the stepmother now living seemed to resent the fact of Jack's existence. His father loved him dearly, but, when the father was away, Jack had a sore time with his sour-tempered stepmother. No wonder he only came home to meals; no wonder he preferred his fairy-tale book to her venomous tongue.

When supper-time came, Jack was always summoned to his food well in time for it to be cleared away before his father came in; and the reason for this was that his father should not see how he was stinted.

But one day the father got to know about these things, and taxed his wife on her treatment of the boy.

'Look here, sir,' said she, 'I wish to goodness you would take your wretched son away and put him in a school for saints, since you think he is so good. As for me, he plagues my life out, and, if you keep him here with his ne'er-do-well ways, you'll come home some evening to find me gone.'

Instead of beating his wife for these words—as some men do when their wives so beseech them—the goodman put his hand on her shoulder and said, 'Nay, nay, my dear; the boy is only a boy; let him stay with us another year until he can fend for himself. Now, I'll tell you what: let the man who looks after the sheep come in here and do the work about the house, and Jack will take his place in the field. The man can have Jack's bed, and Jack will be delighted to sleep in the outhouse. What say you?'

The wife could not object to this, for, at least, the man would be more useful and less troublesome about the house than Jack could ever be. So she agreed to her husband's proposal.

The next day the plan was put into operation.

The man was set to work about the house, and Jack was sent out into the fields to mind the sheep. As he went he sang merrily, for he loved the green fields and the animals. He doubted the dinner his stepmother had put up for him, wrapped in a kitchen clout*; yet he sang merrily as he went in search of the sheep:

> '*Green gravel! Green gravel!*
> *Thy grass is so green.*
> *'Tis the fairies' green gravel*
> *With the daisies between.*'

Then, when he had found them:

> '*Snowy sheepie-woolsides,*
> *Save your wool for me;*
> *Then in snowy yuletides*
> *Snug and warm I'll be.*'

120

*Clout, rag

Then, later, when he began to get hungry, it was:

> *Sheepie, wander, wander*
> *All the fields about ;*
> *Grass is growing under,*
> *Clover budding out.*
> *My mother does not squander*
> *Cakes on me, I doubt ;*
> *What is here, I wonder,*
> *In this kitchen clout ?'*

And, sitting down on a mossy bank, he opened the clout in which his stepmother had wrapped his dinner. Lo and behold, it was dry bread, with a very thick layer of dripping scraped off from it back into the pot. He ate very little, thinking that surely his father would give him something nicer to eat when he got home.

In the afternoon he sat on the hillside watching the sheep and singing merrily, when he saw an aged man with a staff making his way towards him.

'God bless you, son,' said the aged one.

'Good-morrow, father,' replied the boy. 'You are weary. Rest a while on this mossy bank.'

'Ay, I will,' said the old man, sitting down beside the boy. 'You speak truly : I am weary, and hungry, and thirsty too. Have you any food ? And would your young legs take you to the stream to bring me back a draught of water ?'

'I have food, such as it is,' replied Jack readily ; and he offered him the dry bread and scrape that his stepmother had given him. 'As for water, I have a pannikin, and I'll soon fill it at the stream.' And with that he hurried off to fetch the water.

When he returned, and the old man had eaten and drank, he thanked the boy. 'God love you, child,' he said ; 'you have been kind to me. And now, in return, I am minded to grant you three wishes of your heart. Think well, and then name them ; and it shall be as I say.'

THE FRIAR AND THE BOY

Jack thought and thought; but all he could decide on to begin with was a bow and arrow. So he asked for that.

'Certainly!' said the old man; and, rising, he went behind the bank, and presently returned with the bow and arrow, which he gave to the boy.

'This will last you all your life,' he said; 'and it will never break. All you have to do is to draw it with the arrow on the string, and whatever you aim at will fall, pierced by the arrow.'

Jack was delighted, and, in order to test it, he fixed an arrow and let it fly at a hawk passing overhead. The arrow sped and pierced the body of the hawk, which came down plump at their feet.

At this Jack considered his second wish, for he said to himself, 'An old man who can give me a bow and arrow that can never miss, can give me almost anything.' Then he made up his mind and asked for a pipe on which to play tunes.

'I have always wanted a pipe,' he said; 'I would like one so much, no matter how small it is.'

Then the old man got up and went behind the bank, and came back presently with a beautiful pipe, which he gave to the boy.

'It is a strange pipe,' he said. 'When you play upon it any one besides yourself who hears the music must dance, and keep on dancing till the music stops.'

Jack thought this was fine, and would have played a tune there and then, but he looked at the aged man and saw that it would hurt him to dance; so he waited: there was always the 'good Friar' to pipe to.

'Now, child,' said the old man at last, 'what is your third and last wish?'

Jack pondered a long time, and at last he chuckled and clapped his hands with glee. When the old man asked him what tickled him so, he could not reply at once, as he was so busy enjoying some joke beforehand. At last, when he was able to speak, he said, 'Father, it has just crossed my mind that my stepmother is always looking at me sourly and always scolding me. I wish that when she does this she will laugh, and go on laughing till I give her the word to stop.   Can you grant that wish, father?'

'I can,' said the old man; 'and it will be so.   When she looks at you sourly or speaks to you crossly, she will laugh until she falls to the ground, and then go on laughing until you tell her to stop.'

When Jack had thanked him, the old man said good-bye and tottered away, leaning heavily on his staff.   Meanwhile Jack sat and nursed his three wishes, feeling as gay-hearted about his good luck as a lambkin with three tails.

When the sun set at last and his day's work was done, he rose and trudged homewards in great glee.   As he went he played his pipe, and all the sheep and cattle and horses and dogs danced, till he left off for laughing at the sight of them kicking up their heels. Even the birds and the bees waltzed in the air, and, as he crossed a bridge, he saw the little fishes pirouetting in the stream below.

As soon as he reached home he put the pipe away, and, going into the house, found his father at supper.

'Father,' said he, 'I am terribly hungry after looking to the sheep all day; and, besides, my dinner was very dry.'

'Here you are, my son,' replied his father; and, cutting a wing from the roast capon on the table before him, he set it on a plate and pushed it over to the boy.

At this the stepmother, grudging to see such a nice portion given to the boy, turned upon him with a look that would have made a cow give sour milk.   Then, on the instant, she burst out laughing. Her husband stared at her in amazement, but still she laughed, her sides shaking with her shrill peals; and louder and louder she laughed, until the rafters shook and she fell to the ground, still laughing as if she would die of it.

At last Jack, with his capon's wing in both hands before him, stopped eating to cry, 'Enough, I say!'   And immediately the stepmother ceased her laughter and struggled to her feet, looking more dead than alive.

Now, the next day, when Jack was minding the sheep, the good

Friar called at the house, and the stepmother told him what a naughty boy Jack was, and how he had made her laugh till she had nearly died, and then mocked her.

'Go you, now,' she said; 'go and find him in the fields and give him a sound beating for my sake. It will do him good—and me too.'

So the Friar went out into the fields and at last found the boy, with his bow and arrow in his hands.

'Young man,' said the Friar, 'tell me at once what you have done to your stepmother that she is so angered with you. Tell me at once, I say, or I will give you a sound beating.'

'What's the matter with you?' replied Jack. 'If my stepmother wants me beaten, let her do it herself. See that bird?' He pointed to a very plump bird flying overhead. 'If you fetch it when it drops, you can have it.'

With this he let fly an arrow and pierced the bird, which fell to earth a little way off in a bramble patch. As the Friar darted forward to get it—for it was indeed a plump bird—Jack drew forth his pipe and began to play.

It is said that he who hops among thorns is either chasing a snake or being chased by one; and it looked as if either the one or the other was the Friar's case, for he hopped high in the bramble bushes and danced as if he had gone mad in both heels at once.

To see the good Friar dancing willy-nilly among the bramble bushes, kicking up his heels to the tune of the pipe, higher still and higher—oh, it was a sight for Jack's eyes, for he loved the Friar to distraction in less ways than one. So long as Jack piped, the Friar danced. His dress was torn to shreds, but that seemed a small matter. The thorns did admirable work, but the Friar did not care. On with the dance! *Tara-tara-tara-ra-ra*—the Friar seemed to be enjoying himself, though more for Jack's benefit than his own. Faster and faster shrilled the pipe, and faster danced the Friar, until at last he fell down among the brambles, a sorry spectacle, still kicking his feet in the air to the merry rhythm. Then Jack ceased piping, but only to laugh; for he had small pity for the Friar.

'Friend Jack!' cried the Friar, gathering himself up, 'forbear, I pray you. I am nigh to death. Permit me to depart and I will be your friend for ever.'

'Get up and go, then,' cried Jack, 'before I begin to play again.'

The good Friar needed no further permission. What remnant of a robe was left him he gathered up, and fled to his own home. There he clothed himself decently and made all haste to Jack's parents.

When they saw his woebegone countenance they questioned him closely.

'I have been with your son,' he replied. 'Grammercy! By these scratches on my face, and by others you cannot see, he is in league with the Evil One, or I am no holy Friar. He played a tune on his pipe and I danced—danced!—think of it! And all in the bramble bushes! Your son is plainly lost; I hesitate to think what it will cost you to save his soul from the devil's clutch.'

'Here is a fine thing,' exclaimed the wife, turning to her husband. 'This your son has nearly killed the holy Father!'

'Benedicite!' said the good man fervently, and the Friar wondered for a moment what he meant exactly.

When Jack returned home his father at once asked him what he had been doing. He replied that he had been having a merry time with the good Friar, who was so fond of music that he could dance to it anywhere—among bramble bushes for preference. These saints, of course——

'But what music is this you play?' broke in his father, who was growing vastly interested. 'I should like to hear it.'

'Heaven forfend!' cried the Friar, getting uneasy.

'Yes, yes; I should like to hear it,' persisted his father.

'Then, if that is so, and you must hear his accursed tune, I beg that you will bind me to the door-post so that I cannot move. I have had more than enough of it.'

They took him at his word and bound him securely to the door-post; so that he was, so to speak, out of the dance when Jack took his pipe and began to play.

Then had you seen a merry spectacle! At the first notes the good man and his wife began to tread a sprightly measure, while the Friar, bound fast to the post, squirmed and wriggled, showing plainly that he would foot it if he could, and dispense with the brambles for once.

As the piping went on, the merry measure became a tarantelle. The staid old folks threw off their age, and kicked their heels high in the air. Faster and faster went the music; wilder and wilder grew the dance. The Friar burst his bonds and joined in. Nothing was safe: chairs were hustled into the fire; the table was pushed this way and that, and the lighted lamp upon it was rocking.

Seeing the fury of the thing, Jack got up and led the way out into the street, still piping. They followed; the neighbours flocked out and joined in the dance; even those who had gone to bed rushed down, and all followed at Jack's heels down the village street, dancing madly to his wild piping. People jostled and fell and went on dancing on all fours, but the Friar kept his feet, if not his head, and whirled many a maid into the thick of it.

At length, when they had reached the village green, and the scene had become one of indescribable confusion and abandon, Jack's father drew near him and said, as he whirled by: 'Jack! if you have any consideration for your poor old father, for heaven's sake, stop!'

Now the boy loved his father; so, on hearing these words, he ceased his piping. Suddenly all came to a standstill. There was a rapid melting away as if people had awakened from a dream in which they had been making themselves ridiculous. And, in the midst of this, came forward the Friar with Jack's stepmother in close attendance.

'That cursèd boy!' cried he, shaking his fist at Jack. 'See here, my fine fellow, you cannot do this kind of thing with impunity.

THE FRIAR AND THE BOY

I hereby summon you before the Judge next Friday, and see to it that you appear in person to answer the charges I shall bring against you.'

At this the boy raised his pipe again to his lips; but, before he could blow a single note, they had all taken to their heels in dismay, leaving him standing there alone in the empty square.

It was Friday, and the Judge, be-wigged and severe, sat on the bench, with all the appearance of a great case before him. The Friar was there as prosecutor; the King's Proctor was watching the case—in case; the Public Persuader was there with his suave and well-paid manner, admonishing all sides; Jack's parents and all his relations and friends were there, wondering greatly whether Jack, who stood in the dock, would live to tell the tale of what death was meted out to him.

'M'lud!' said the Friar when there was silence in court; 'I have brought before you a wicked boy who, by associating with the Evil One, has corrupted the manners of this community, and brought sorrow and trouble to all. Though young he is none the less a wizard, having infernal skill.'

'Ay, that he is,' put in the stepmother. 'He is in league—in league——' But she got no further, for, in a trice, she was laughing as none had ever been known to laugh.

The Judge was scandalised.

'Woman!' he said. 'This Court itself has been known to laugh, but this behaviour on your part is unseemly.'

'Stop it!' said Jack from the dock, and he spoke short and sharp.

She ceased immediately, and then the Judge requested her to tell her tale; but she was so exhausted that the Friar had to tell it for her.

'M'lud,' he said, 'it is simply this: the prisoner here has a pipe, and, when he plays upon it, all who hear must dance themselves to death, whether they like it or not.'

'Ah!' said the Judge, ' I should like to hear this Dance of Death.

You have heard it, good father, and you still live. Maybe, when I have heard it, I shall be charmed, like the serpent, and come out to be killed at once. Let him play his music.'

And, with this remark, the Judge sat back, while Jack took up his pipe to play.

'Stop! stop!' cried the Friar in dismay. But Jack heeded not. At the nod of the Judge he started up a merry tune, and immediately the whole Court began to imagine itself a ballroom. Set to partners—cross—ladies' chain—chassé! It was a regular whirl as the boy piped faster and faster. The Judge himself leapt down from the bench and joined in, holding up his robes and footing it merrily. But, when he bruised his shins severely against the clerk's desk, he yelled for the boy to cease piping.

'Yes, I will,' cried Jack, and as he paused with his pipe raised to his lips they all waited on his words: 'I will, if they will all promise to treat me properly from this time forward.'

'I think,' said the Judge, 'if you will put your pipe away, they will consent to an amicable arrangement.'

Then he climbed back to the bench and sat himself down, and put on his considering cap to pass sentence.

There was silence in court for some minutes. Then came in solemn tones:

'Judgment for the defendant—with costs!'

And so, all parties being satisfied, the Court adjourned, and every one went home to supper quite happy.

THE GREEN SERPENT

A FRENCH FAIRY TALE

THERE was once upon a time a very great Queen who gave birth to little twin girls. She immediately sent out invitations to twelve fairies in the neighbouring countries to come to the feast according to the custom of the country—a custom that was never by any means overlooked, because it was such a great advantage to have the fairies as guests.

When the twelve fairies were all assembled in the great hall where the feast was to be held, they took their seats at the table—a very big table laden with such good things to eat, and so rich, that it was past all comprehension. No sooner had all the guests seated themselves, than who should enter but the wicked fairy Magotine!

Now the Queen, when she saw her, felt that some disaster would follow because she had omitted to send this fairy an invitation; but she hid the thought deep in her mind, and off she went and found a beautiful soft seat all embroidered in gold and inlaid with sapphires; then all the other fairies moved up and made room for Magotine to seat herself, saying at the same time, 'Hurry up, sister, and make your wish for the little Princesses, and then come and sit down.'

But, before Magotine came to table, she said rudely that she was quite big enough to eat standing. There she made a great mistake, because the table was very high and Magotine was very small, and, in reaching up, she fell. This misfortune only increased her bad temper.

'Madam,' said the Queen, 'I beg you to be seated at table.'

'If you had so much wished to see me here,' replied the fairy, 'you would have sent me an invitation the same as the others. You have only invited to your court the most beautiful, well-dressed and good-tempered fairies, like my sisters here. With them I have no fault to find; I, however, have one advantage over them, as you will see!'

Then all the fairies begged her to seat herself with them, and she did so. In front of each fairy was placed a beautiful bouquet made of all kinds of precious stones. Each took the bouquet immediately in front of her, and there remained none at all for Magotine; and she growled furiously between her teeth.

The Queen, quickly noticing the awful error, ran to her cabinet and came back with a large cup all perfumed and studded outside with rubies, and inside full of diamonds that gave forth a thousand different colours. Going up to Magotine, she begged her to receive the present. But Magotine only shook her head and replied: 'Keep your jewels, madam, I do not want them. I came simply to see if you had thought of me, and I find that you have forgotten me altogether.' And with this she gave a tap with her wand on the table and at once all the good things were turned into serpents, which wriggled about and hissed viciously. The other fairies, seeing this, were filled with horror; they threw down their serviettes* and quitted the table.

While they were leaving the table the wicked little fairy Magotine, who had come to disturb the peace, made her way to the room where the little Princesses were asleep in a golden cot covered with a canopy studded with diamonds, the most beautiful ever seen in the world. The other fairies followed her to watch. Magotine stopped beside the cot, and, taking out her wand quickly, she touched one of the little Princesses, saying at the same time: 'I wish that you become the most ugly person that it would be possible to find.' Then she turned to the other little Princess; but, before she could do anything further, the other fairies interfered, and taking a great pan full of vitriol,** threw it over the wicked Magotine. But not a drop touched her, for, before it splashed upon the floor, she had disappeared before their very eyes.

The Queen then made her way to the cot and took out the little

---

Serviettes, table napkins
**Vitriol*, sulfuric acid

Princess that Magotine had wished to be so ugly; and the Queen cried with sorrow because, every minute as she looked at it, the child was becoming uglier and uglier, until at last any one could see she was the ugliest baby in the world.

Now the other good fairies consulted amongst themselves how they could lighten this great sorrow, so they turned to the Queen and said: 'Madam, it is not possible to undo the evil that the fairy Magotine has put upon your child, but we will wish for her something that will help to balance that evil.' And then they told the Queen that one day her daughter would be extremely happy. With this the fairies took their departure, but not before the Queen had given them all some beautiful presents; for this custom goes on amongst all the peoples of the earth, and will continue when other customs are forgotten.

The Queen called her ugly daughter Laideronnette, and the beautiful daughter Bellote; and these names suited them perfectly, because Laideronnette was frightfully ugly, and her sister was equally charming and beautiful.

When Laideronnette was twelve years old, she went and threw herself at the feet of the King and Queen, and begged them to allow her to go and shut herself up in a castle far away near the Light of Dawn, and to let her take the necessary servants and food to live there. She reminded them that they still had Bellote, and that she was enough to console them.

After a long while they agreed, and Laideronnette went away to her castle near the Light of Dawn. On one side of the castle the sea came right up to the window, and on another there was a great canal; from still another view was a vast forest as far as the eye could see, and beyond again a great desert.

The little Princess played musical instruments beautifully, and also had a sweet voice just like a bird, and sang divinely; and so, with these delights, she lived for two whole years in perfect solitude. Then, at the end of the two years, she began to feel homesick and wished to see her father and mother, the King and Queen; so she started on the journey home at once, and arrived just as her sister the Princess Bellote was going to be married.

Now as soon as they saw Laideronnette, they did not offer to kiss her or say they were pleased to see her; and they told her she was not to come to the marriage feast, nor to the ball afterwards. Poor little Laideronnette said she had not come to dance and be merry; neither had she come to the marriage feast; she had come because she felt homesick and wanted to see her father and mother. However, she would go away back to her castle near the Light of Dawn, for there the desert, the trees, and the fountains never reproached her with her ugliness when she came near them.

The King and Queen were sorry that they had been so unkind, and asked Laideronnette to remain two or three days; but Laideronnette was so upset that she refused. Then her sister Bellote gave her some silk, and Bellote's betrothed gave her some ribbons. Now, if Laideronnette had been like some people she would have thrown the silk and the ribbons at the Princess and her future husband. But Laideronnette was not like that, and she only felt a great sorrow in her little heart, and turned away and took her faithful nurse with her; and all the way home towards the Light of Dawn, Laideronnette never spoke a single word.

One day, when Laideronnette was walking in a very shaded valley in the forest, she saw on a tree a big green serpent, who lifted his head and said to her, 'Laideronnette, you are not the only unhappy person; look at my horrible form, and I was born more beautiful than you.' The Princess was so terrified to hear a serpent talk that she fled away and remained in her room for days, in case she should see or meet the green serpent again.

Eventually Laideronnette got tired of being shut up in her room all day alone, so one evening she came down and went to the edge of the sea, bewailing all the time her awful loneliness and her sad destiny, when suddenly she saw coming towards her over the waves a little barque of a thousand different colours and designs on its sides. The sail was beautifully embroidered in gold, and the

Princess became very curious to see all the beauties that the barque must contain inside.

She made her way aboard. Inside she found it lined with lovely velvet, the seats of pure gold and the walls studded with diamonds; then, all of a sudden, the barque turned and went out to sea. The Princess ran up and caught hold of the oars, thinking to get back to her castle; but it was no use: she could do nothing at all. On and on went the barque and the poor little Princess wept bitterly at this new sorrow that had come to her.

'Magotine is doing me a bad turn again,' she thought, so she abandoned herself to her fate, hoping that she would die. 'Just after I was looking forward to a little pleasure in seeing my parents yesterday, comes one catastrophe on another; and now my sister is going to be married to a great Prince. What have I done that I should have to live alone in a desert spot because of my ugliness? Alas! for my company I have only a serpent—who speaks!'

These reflections brought tears from the Princess, and she gazed on every side to see which way death was coming for her. While looking and gazing she saw, approaching on the waves, a serpent, flashing green in the sunlight. He came up to the side of the barque and said: 'If you are good enough to receive help from a poor Green Serpent, tell me, for I am in a position to save your life.'

'Death is nothing to me compared to the sight of you,' cried the Princess; 'and, if you really want to do me a favour, never show yourself before my eyes again.'

The Green Serpent gave a big sigh (for that is the way of serpents in love), and, without replying at all, he dived to the bottom of the sea.

'What a horrible monster!' said the Princess to herself. 'His body is of a thousand green colours, and he has eyes like fire. I would rather die than that *he* should save my life. What love can he have for me, and by what right does he speak like a human being?'

Suddenly a voice replied to her thoughts, and it said, 'Listen,

Laideronnette, it is not my fault that I am a Green Serpent; and it will not be for ever; but, I assure you, I am less ugly in my special way than you are in yours. All the same, it is not my wish to pain you; I would comfort you if you would only let me!'

The voice surprised the Princess very much, so sweet was it that she could not hold back her tears. 'I am not crying because I am afraid to die,' she answered, 'but I am hurt enough to weep over my ugliness. I have nothing to live for, why should I cry for fear of dying?'

While she was thus moralising, the little barque that floated with the wind ran into a rock and broke up into pieces, and, when all else had sunk, there remained of the wreck only two little pieces of wood. The poor Princess caught hold of these two little pieces and kept herself afloat; then, happily, her feet touched a rock and she scrambled up on to it.

Alas! what was that coming towards her now but the Green Serpent! As if he knew that she was afraid, he moved away a little, and said: 'You would be less afraid of me, Laideronnette, if you knew what advantages can be had through me; it is one of the punishments of my destiny, however, that I should frighten every one in the world.'

And with this he threw himself back into the sea, and Laideronnette remained alone on the rock in the middle of the ocean. On whichever side she looked she saw nothing but what would cause her despair; and darkness began to fall, and she had no food to eat, and Laideronnette did not know where to sleep.

'I thought,' said she sadly, 'that I should end my days at the bottom of the sea; but without a doubt this is to be the end; what sea-monster will come to eat me up?'

She crept higher and higher up the rock, and looked out over the sea. Darkness was falling fast, so she took off her dress and covered her head and face in it, so that she could not see the awful things that would pass in the night.

After a long time she fell asleep, and dreamt that she heard the most melodious music, and she tried to persuade herself that she was awake, but in a second she heard a voice singing, as if to her alone :—

> *'Suffer the love that wounds you :*
>   *It is a tender fire.*
> *The love that follows and surrounds you*
>   *To your love would aspire.*
> *Banish fear, forgo all grieving :*
> *Love hath joys past all believing.*
>   *Suffer the love that wounds you :*
>   *It is a tender fire.'*

At the end of this song she woke up at once. 'What happiness or what misfortune threatens me?' said she. She opened her eyes very carefully, for she was full of fear, expecting to find herself surrounded by monsters from the sea ; but, imagine her surprise to find herself in a chamber all glittering with gold! The bed on which she lay was perfect, and the most beautiful to be seen anywhere in the wide world. Laideronnette got up and went out on to a wide balcony, where she saw all the beauties of nature before her. The gardens were full of flowers—flowers that gave out the rarest perfume ; fountains splashed everywhere, and were surmounted by lovely figures ; and outside the gardens was a wonderful forest green with verdure. The palace and the walls were encrusted with precious stones, the roofs and ceilings were made of pearls, so beautifully done that it was a perfect work of art. From the tower of the palace could be seen beyond the forest a sea calm and placid, just like a sheet of glass, and on the sea floated thousands of little boats with all kinds of different sails, which, when caught by the wind, had the most lovely effect imaginable.

'Gods, sweet gods!' cried Laideronnette, 'what do I see? Where am I? Is it possible that I am in heaven—I who yesterday was in peril in a barque?' She walked as she spoke, then she stopped ; what noise was that she heard in her apartment? She turned and entered her room, and, coming towards her, she saw a hundred little animated pagodas, all of different designs. Some were very beautiful, while others were extremely ugly. In fact there was hardly any difference between the little pagodas and the people who inhabit the world.

The pagoda which now presented itself before Laideronnette was the deputy of the King. It said that sometimes it went travelling all over the world, but was allowed to do so only on one condition: namely, that it did not talk to any one; otherwise the King would not give the necessary permission. On its return it entertained the King by recounting all that it had heard and seen; moreover, it held the most precious secrets of the court. 'It will be a pleasure to serve you, madam,' it went on, 'and everything you want we shall be delighted to get for you; in the meantime we will play for you and dance so that you will have plenty to make you happy.' And they all began to dance and sing, and play on castanets and tambourines.

When they had finished, the principal pagoda said to the Princess: 'Listen, madam, these hundred pagodas are here expressly to serve you, and any mortal thing you want in the world you have only to ask for it and it shall be yours at once.' The little pagodas paused in their movements and came near to Laideronnette, and she saw at a glance that they were simply lovely. Looking inside, she saw that they contained presents for her, some useful and others so beautiful that she could only cry out with joy.

The biggest pagoda, which was a little figure of pure diamonds, then came up to Laideronnette and asked her if she would now like her bath in the little grotto. The Princess walked, between a guard of honour, to the place it pointed to, and there she saw two beautiful baths of crystal, and from them came such a lovely fragrance that Laideronnette could not help remarking about it. Then she asked why there were two bathing places, and they told her that one was for her and the other for the King of the Pagodas.

'But where is he, then?' cried Laideronnette.

'Madam,' said they, 'at present he is at the war; but you shall see him on his return.'

The Princess asked them if he was married, and they shook their little top turrets, meaning that he was not. Then they told her that he was so good and kind that he had never found any one good enough to marry.

Laideronnette then undressed herself and got into the bath, and at once the pagodas began to sing and play. Then, when the Princess was ready to come out of her bath, she was given a dress of shining colours, and they all walked before her to her room, where her toilet was made by maids, all of them quaint little pagodas.

The Princess was astounded, and expressed her delight at her great good fortune.

There was not a day that the pagodas did not come and tell her all the news of the courts where they had been in different parts of the world. People plotting for war, others seeking for peace; wives who were unfaithful, old widowers who married wives a thousand times more unsuitable than those they had lost; discovered treasures; favourites at court, and out of it, who had fallen from the coveted seat they occupied; jealous wives, to say nothing at all about husbands; women who flirted, and naughty children;—in fact they told her everything that was going on, to make her happy and to help to pass the time away.

Now one night it happened that the Princess could not sleep, and she lay awake, thinking. At last she said: 'What is going to happen to me? Shall I always be here? My life is passed more happily than I ever could wish; but, all the same, there is a feeling in my heart that there is something missing.'

'Ah! Princess,' said a voice, 'is it not your own fault? If you would only love me, you would recognise at once that it would be possible to remain in this palace for ever, alone with the one you loved, without ever wishing to leave it.'

'Which little pagoda is speaking to me now?' she asked.

'What dreadful counsel to give me, contrary to all I have been taught in my life!'

'It is not a pagoda who is talking to you; it is the unhappy King who loves you, madam.'

'A King who loves me!' replied the Princess. 'Has this King eyes, or does he need glasses? Has he not seen that I am the ugliest person in the world?'

'Yes, I have seen you, madam. All that you are, and all that you may have been, make not the least difference to me. I repeat, I love you.'

The Princess did not speak again, but she spent the rest of the night thinking over this adventure.

Every day on getting up she found new clothes and fresh jewels; it was too much homage, considering she was so ugly.

One night—it must have been the darkest night of the whole year—Laideronnette was asleep, and, on awakening, she felt that some one sat near her bed. The Princess put out her hand to feel, but somebody took her hand and kissed it, and in so doing let tear-drops fall upon it. She knew full well that it must be the invisible King.

'What do you want with me?' she said. 'Can I love somebody I have never seen and do not know?'

'Ah! madam,' replied he, 'what pleasure it would give me to be able to fulfil your wish! But the wicked Magotine, who played you such a cruel trick, has done the same to me, for I am condemned to remain thus for seven years; five have already gone by and there remain another two years. You could, if you would, lessen the time and make it pass quickly for me if you would marry me; you will think that what I ask is impossible; but, madam, if you only knew how deep my love is for you, you would never refuse me the favour I ask of you.'

Laideronnette, as I have already said, thought that this invisible King was very sweet, and the love he offered was without a doubt genuine. And, in a moment of pity, she replied that she would like a few days to think over his proposal. So the days passed, and all the time the music went on and the pagodas danced and new presents arrived for her, better than those she had received before. And in the end the Princess made up her mind to marry the invisible King, and she promised to wait to see him until his time of punishment was over and he could take visible shape again.

Then the voice said: 'The consequences will be terrible for you and for me if your curiosity should overcome you, and I shall have to commence my punishment all over again; but, should you, on the other hand, stay your desire to see me, you will receive that beauty that the wicked Magotine took away from you.'

The Princess, full of this new hope, promised to keep her word to him. But after a while she had a deep desire to see her father and mother again; also her sister and her husband. The pagodas, who knew the road well, conducted the royal family to the castle of Laideronnette's father and mother; and when she saw them she nearly died of joy.

Her mother and her sister questioned Laideronnette about her husband, and Laideronnette remembered what her husband had told her; she did not like to tell her people the truth, so she told them that he was at the war fighting, and that he did not like seeing people. But her mother and sister chaffed her about him, and at last Laideronnette said that the wicked Magotine had punished him for seven years, that two remained to be finished, and that she had married him without ever having seen him; but that he was a charming person and his conversation proved the fact, and that if she held her curiosity until the two years were up, she would regain all the beauty that the fairy Magotine had taken from her.

'Ah!' replied her mother, 'is it possible that you are such a simpleton as to believe all those tales? Your husband is a huge monster; he is the King of monkeys truly.'

'I know full well,' replied Laideronnette, 'that he is the god of Love himself.'

'What a terrible mistake!' screamed the Queen Bellote.

The poor Princess was so confused and upset that, after giving them the presents, she resolved to go and see her husband. Ah, fatal curiosity! She took a little lamp with her that she might be able to see him the better. What was her surprise when, instead of Love, she saw the Green Serpent! He drew himself up in rage and sorrow:

'O wicked one!' cried he; 'is this the return for all my love for you?'

Now Magotine, knowing that Laideronnette and the Green Serpent were in trouble, came to add to their sorrow and taunt them. She took away, with one wave of her wand, all the lovely castles and fountains and gardens. And Laideronnette, seeing all that she had done, was very troubled. So, during the night, Laideronnette deplored her sad fate. Then, high up near the stars, she saw coming towards her the Green Serpent.

'I always make you afraid,' he cried; 'but you are infinitely dear to me.'

'Is it you, Serpent, dear lover; is it you?' cried Laideronnette. 'Can you forgive me for my fatal curiosity?'

'Ah! how the sorrow of absence troubles this loving heart!' replied the Serpent, with never a word of reproach to Laideronnette for her broken promise.

Magotine, now, was one of those fairies who never slept at all: the wish to do harm and never to miss the chance kept her awake; and she did not fail to hear the conversation between the King Serpent and his spouse; and she came down upon them in a fury.

'Now then, Green Serpent,' said she, 'I order you for your punishment to go right to the good Proserpine, and give her my compliments.'

The poor Green Serpent went at once with great sighs, leaving the Queen in sorrow. And Laideronnette cried out:

'What crime have we committed now, you wicked Magotine? I am certain that the poor King, whom you have sent to the bottomless pit of hell, was as innocent as I myself am; but let me die: it is the least you can do.'

'You would be too happy,' said Magotine, 'were I to listen and grant you your wish. I will send you to the bottom of the sea.' So saying, she took the poor Princess to the top of the highest mountain and tied a mill-stone about her neck, telling her that she was to go down and bring enough Water of Discretion to fill up her great big glass. The Princess said that it was absolutely impossible to carry all that water.

'If you do not,' said Magotine, 'you may rest assured that your Green Serpent will suffer more.'

This threat caused the Queen to think of her utter feebleness. She began to walk, but, alas! it was useless. Oh! if the Fairy Protectress would only help her! Loudly she called, and lo! there stood the good fairy by her side.

'See,' said she, 'to what a pass your fatal curiosity has brought you!' So saying, she took her to the top of the mountain; she gave her a little carriage drawn by two white mice and told them to descend the mountain. Then she gave the little mice a vessel to fill up with the Water of Discretion for Magotine, and produced a little pair of iron shoes for Laideronnette to put on. She counselled her not to remain on the mountain and not to stay by the fountain, but to go into a little wood and to remain there three years, for then Magotine would think that she was getting the water or that she had perished in the awful perils of the voyage.

Laideronnette kissed and embraced the good Fairy Protectress, and thanked her a thousand times for her great favours. 'But, madam,' said Laideronnette, 'all the joys that you have given me will not lessen the sorrow of not having my Green Serpent.'

'He will come to you after you have been three years in the wood in the mountain,' said the fairy; 'and on your return you can give the water to Magotine.'

Laideronnette promised the fairy not to forget anything she had told her. So, when she got into her carriage, the mice took her to get the water, and afterwards they went to the wood that the fairy had told them about. There never was a more lovely place. Fruit hung on all the branches; and there were long avenues where the sun could not pierce; thousands of little fountains splashed, but the most wonderful thing of all was, that all the animals could speak.

Three years passed, and the time had now arrived for her departure with the water for Magotine. So Laideronnette told all the animals that she was sorry to leave them, and tears fell from her eyes, because she was so touched with the kindness they all had shown her.

She did not forget the vessel full of the Water of Discretion, nor the little shoes of iron that the good fairy had given her; and, just when Magotine thought her dead, she presented herself all of a sudden before her, the stones around her neck, the shoes of iron on her feet, and the vessel full of water in her hand.

Magotine on seeing her cried out in surprise. Where had she come from?

'Madam,' said Laideronnette, 'I passed three years in trying to get this water for you.'

Magotine roared with laughter when she thought of the awful job this poor Queen must have had to get it; but she regarded her attentively.

'What is it that I see?' she cried to Laideronnette, who had changed greatly. 'How did you become so beautiful?'

Laideronnette told her that she had washed in the Water of Discretion, and that was how she had become beautiful.

Magotine, on hearing this, threw the water on the ground. 'I will be avenged,' said she. 'Go down to the bottomless pit and ask Proserpine to give you the Essence of Long Life for me; I am always afraid of falling ill and dying. When you have done this you will be free. But mind you do not upset any; neither may you drink the tiniest drop.

The poor Queen, on hearing this new order, was terribly cut up. She began to cry; and Magotine, seeing this, was delighted. 'Go on, get away!' said she. 'Do not lose one moment.'

THE GREEN SERPENT

Laideronnette walked for a long time without finding the right path, turning first one way and then the other; then suddenly she saw the Fairy Protectress, who said to her:

'Do you know, beautiful Queen, that by the orders of Magotine your husband is to remain as he is until you take the Essence of Life to that wicked fairy?'

'I am yet a long way away,' said Laideronnette.

'Here,' said the Fairy Protectress, 'see, here is a branch of a tree: touch the earth and repeat this verse distinctly.'

The Queen once again kissed the knees of this really good and generous fairy, and at the same time repeated after her:

> *'Thou who all malice canst disarm,*
> *Protect me as I rove!*
> *Deliver me from all who harm,*
> *But not from him I love.*
> *For, if devoured I am to be,*
> *He is my monster—none but he!'*

And immediately, in answer to her prayer, a little boy more beautiful than any in heaven or earth came up to her. On his head was a garland of flowers, and in his hand a bow and arrow. The Queen knew at once that it was Love. He said to her:

'You appeal to me so tenderly that I deserted the heavens.'

Love, who sang beautifully in verse, gave three knocks while singing this song:

> *'Earth, listen and my voice obey.*
> *It is Love who speaks: reveal the way!'*

The earth obeyed: a path opened up, and Love took Laideronnette under his protection; and so they arrived at the mouth of hell. She expected to see her husband in the form of a serpent, but he had just finished his terrible punishment. The first thing that Laideronnette saw was indeed her husband; but she had never seen such a charming figure, nor any one so handsome;

and neither had he seen any one so beautiful as she had become. Then the Queen said with extreme tenderness:

> *'Destiny! I bend the knee*
> *To thee and thy decree:*
> *If he must dwell in deepest hell*
> *He dwelleth there with me,*
> *For e'en in hell I'll love him well*
> *For all eternity.'*

The King was full of joy and love, and showed it by the way he kissed her. Love, however, never did believe in wasting time, so he took the Queen to Proserpine. The Queen gave the compliments of the fairy Magotine, and begged her to give her the Essence of Long Life. Love took it and handed it to her, telling her not to forget the penalty that she had paid for her curiosity, and to take every care this time. He would never leave them again. He conducted them to the fairy Magotine, and then, so that Magotine should not see him, he hid in their hearts.

During this time the fairy Magotine was so impressed with the beauty of human feelings, that she received the poor unfortunate King and Queen with some feeling of generosity. She gave them back the lovely palace with all the good things that they had before, and made the King head of the pagodas again. So they went home, and all the great sorrows that they had passed through they soon forgot in the greater joy of each other.

URASHIMA TARO

A VERY long time ago there lived in Japan a young fisherman named Urashima Taro. His father before him had been a very expert fisherman, but Urashima's skill in the art so far exceeded that of his father, that his name as a fisher was known far and wide beyond his own little village. It was a common saying that he could catch more fish in a day than a dozen others could in a whole week.

But it was not only as a fisher that Urashima excelled. Wherever he was known, he was loved for his kindly heart. Never had he hurt even the meanest creature. Indeed, had it not been necessary to catch fish for his living, he would always have fished with a straight hook, so as to catch only such fish as wished to be caught. And as for teasing and tormenting animals, when he was a boy, his tenderness towards all the dumb creation was a matter for laughter with his companions; but nothing would ever induce him to join in the cruel sport in which some boys delight.

One evening, as Urashima was returning from a hard day's fishing, he met a number of boys all shouting and laughing over something they were worrying in the middle of the road. It was a tortoise they had caught and were ill-treating. Between them all, what with sticks and stones and other kinds of torture, the poor creature was hard beset and seemed almost frightened to death.

Urashima could not bear to see a helpless thing treated in that way, so he interfered.

'Boys!' he said, 'that's no way to treat a harmless dumb creature. You'll kill the poor thing!'

145

But the boys merely laughed, and, taking no further notice, continued their cruel sport.

'What's a tortoise?' cried one. 'Besides, it's great fun. Come on, lads!' And they went on with their heartless game.

Urashima thought the matter over for a little, wondering how he could persuade the boys to give the tortoise up to him. At last he said with a smile, 'Come, boys! I know you're good-hearted young fellows: I'll make a bargain with you. What I really wanted was to buy the tortoise,—that is, if it is your own.'

'Of course it's our own. We caught it.' They had begun to gather round him at the prospect of a sale, for they relished the money to buy sweetmeats even more than the cruel sport of tormenting an innocent creature.

'Very well,' replied Urashima, bringing a string of coins out of his pocket and holding them up. 'See! you can buy a lot of nice things with this. What do you say?'

He smiled at them so sweetly and spoke so gently that, with the cash dangling before their eyes, they were soon won over. The biggest boy then grabbed the tortoise, and held it out to him with one hand, while he reached for the string of coins with the other. 'All right, uncle,' he said, 'you can have the tortoise.'

Urashima handed over the money in exchange for the poor, frightened creature, and the boys were soon making their way to the nearest sweetmeat shop.

Meanwhile Urashima looked at the tortoise, which looked back at him with wistful eyes full of meaning ; and, though it could not speak, the young fisherman understood it perfectly, and his tender heart went out to it.

'Poor little tortoise!' he said, holding it up and stroking it gently to soothe its fears, 'you are all right with me. But remember, sweet little one, you've had a narrow squeak of losing a very long life. How long is it ? Ten thousand years, they say ;— that's ten times as long as a stork can boast of. Now I'm going to take you right back to the sea, so that you can swim away to your home and to your own people.   But promise me you will never let yourself be caught again.'

The tortoise promised with its eyes.   So wistful and grateful were they, that Urashima felt he could never forget them.

By this time he was down on the seashore, and there he placed the tortoise in the sea and watched it swim away.   Then he went home feeling very happy about the whole thing.

Morning was breaking when Urashima pushed off his boat for his day's fishing.   The sea was calm, and the air was full of the soft, sweet warmth of summer.   Soon he was out skimming over the blue depths, and when the tide began to ebb, he drifted far beyond the other fishermen's boats, until his own was lost to their sight.

It was such a lovely morning when the sun rose and slanted across the waters, that, when he thought of the short span of human life, he wished that he had thousands of years to live, like the tortoise he had rescued from the boys the day before.

As he was dreaming these thoughts, he was suddenly startled by a sweet voice calling his name.   It fell on his ears like the note of a silver bell dropping from the skies.   Again it came, nearer than before:

'Urashima! Urashima!'

He looked all around on the surface of the sea, thinking that some one had hailed him from a boat, but there was no one there, as far as the eye could reach.

And now he heard the voice again close at hand, and, looking over the side of the boat, he saw a tortoise looking up at him, and he knew by its eyes that it was the same tortoise he had restored to the sea the previous day.

'So we meet again,' he said pleasantly.   'Fancy you finding me in the middle of the ocean!   What is it, you funny little tortoise?   Do you want to be caught again, eh?'

'I have looked for you,' replied the tortoise, 'ever since dawn, and when I saw you in the boat I swam after you to thank you for saving my life.'

'Well, that's very nice of you to say that. I haven't much to offer you, but if you would like to come up into the boat and dry your back in the sun we can have a chat.'

The tortoise was pleased to accept the invitation, and Urashima helped it up over the side. Then, after talking of many things, the tortoise remarked, 'I suppose you have never seen Rin Gin, the Dragon Sea-King's palace, have you?'

Urashima shook his head.

'No,' he replied. 'They tell me it is a beautiful sight, but in all the years that I have spent upon the sea I have never been invited to the Dragon King's palace. It's some distance from here, isn't it?'

'I do not think you believe there is such a place,' replied the tortoise, who had seen a twinkle in Urashima's eye. 'Yet I assure you it exists, but a long way off—right down at the bottom of the sea. If you would really like to see Rin Gin, I will take you there.'

'That is very kind of you,' said Urashima with a polite bow, which pleased the tortoise greatly; 'but I am only a man, you know, and cannot swim a long way under the sea like a tortoise.'

But the little creature hastened to reassure him.

'That's not at all necessary,' it said. 'I'll do the swimming and you can ride on my back.'

Urashima laughed. The idea of his riding on the back of a tortoise that he could hold in his hand was funny, and he said so.

'Never mind how funny it is,' said the tortoise; 'just get on and see.' And then, as Urashima looked at it, the tortoise grew and grew and grew until its back was big enough for two men to ride upon.

'What an extraordinary thing!' exclaimed Urashima. 'Right you are, friend tortoise, I'll come with you.' And with that he jumped on.

'That's better,' said the tortoise; 'now we'll be off. Hold tight!'

The next moment the tortoise plunged into the sea, and dived down and down until Urashima thought they would never be able to reach the surface again in a thousand years. At last he caught sight of a land below them, shining all green with the filtered sunlight; and now, as they took a level course, he could make out the towns and villages below, with beautiful gardens full of bright flowers and waving dreamy trees. Then they passed over a vast green plain, at the further side of which, in a village at the foot of high mountains, shone the splendid portals of a magnificent palace.

'See!' said the tortoise, 'that is the entrance to Rin Gin. We shall soon be there now. How do you feel?'

'Quite well, thank you!' And indeed, when Urashima felt his clothes he found they were quite dry, which was really not so surprising because, as he was borne swiftly through the water, there was all the time a space of air around him, so that not only was he kept quite dry, but he could breathe quite easily.

When they drew nearer to the great gate, Urashima could see beyond it, half hidden by the trees, the shining domes of the palace. It was indeed a magnificent place, unlike anything ever seen in the lands above the sea.

Now they were at the great gate, and the tortoise stopped at the foot of a flight of coral steps and asked him to dismount.

'You can walk now, Urashima'; and it led the way. Then the gatekeeper—a royal sturgeon—challenged them, but the tortoise explained that Urashima was a mortal from the great kingdom of Japan, who had come to visit the Sea King, and the gatekeeper immediately showed them in.

As they advanced, they were met by the courtiers and officials. The dolphin, the bonito, the great cuttle-fish, the bright-red bream; and the mullet, the sole, the flounder, and a host of other fishes came forward and bowed gracefully before the tortoise; indeed, such homage did they pay that Urashima wondered what sway the tortoise held in this kingdom beneath the sea. Then, when the visitor was introduced, they all cried out a welcome. And the dolphin, who was a high official, remarked, 'We are delighted to see so distinguished a stranger from the great kingdom of Japan. Welcome to the palace of the Dragon King of the Sea!'

Then all the fishes went in a procession before them to the interior of the palace.

Now the humble fisherman had never been in such a magnificent place before. He had never read *How to behave in a Palace*, but, though much amazed, he did not feel at all shy. As he followed his guides, he suddenly noticed that the tortoise had disappeared, but he soon forgot this when he saw a lovely Princess, surrounded by her maidens, come forward to greet him.

She was more beautiful than anything on earth, and her robes of pink and green changed colour like the surface of the sea at sunset in some sheltered cove. There were threads of pure gold in her long hair, and, as she smiled, her teeth looked like little white pearls. She spoke soft words to him, and her voice was as the murmur of the sea.

Urashima was so enchanted that he could not speak a word; but he had heard that one must always bow low to a Princess, and he was about to do so when the Princess tripped to his side, and, taking his hand in hers, led him off into a splendid apartment, where she conducted him to the place of honour and asked him to be seated.

'Listen to me, Urashima,' she said in a low, sweet voice. 'I am filled with joy at welcoming you to my father's palace, and I will tell you why. Yesterday you saved the precious life of a tortoise. Urashima, I was that tortoise! It was my life that you saved!'

Urashima could not believe this at first, but, when he gazed into her beautiful eyes, he remembered their wistful look, and her sweet words were spoken in the same voice as that which had called his name upon the sea. And he was so astonished that he could not speak.

'Would you like to live here always, Urashima,—to live in everlasting youth, never growing tired or weary? This is the land of eternal summer, where all is joy, and neither death nor sorrow may come. Stay, Urashima, and I, the Princess of my father's kingdom, will be your bride!'

THE STORY OF URASHIMA TARO

"Urashima was so enchanted that he could not speak a word."

Page 150

THE FIRE BIRD

"There he found the Princess asleep and saw that her face
was the face he had seen in the portrait."

Page 165

Urashima felt it was all a dream; yet, if it were, then from the very heart of that dream he replied in words that came of their own accord.

'Sweet Princess, if I could thank you ten thousand times I should still want to thank you all over again. I will stay here; nay—more: I simply cannot go, for this is the most wonderful place I have ever dreamed of, and you are the most wonderful thing in it.'

A smile spread over her lovely face. She bent towards him, and their lips met in the first sweet kiss of love.

Then, as if by this a magic button had been pressed, a loud gong sounded, and immediately the whole palace was in a bustle of excitement. Presently a procession of all kinds of fishes came in, all richly attired in flowing robes of various colours. Each one advanced with slow and stately pace, some bearing beautiful flowers, others great mother-of-pearl dishes laden with all the delicacies that go to make a feast; others bore trays of coral, red and white, with fragrant wines and rare fruits such as only grow at the bottom of the sea. It was the wedding feast, and with all decorum they set everything before the bride and bridegroom.

It was a day of great joy, a day of song and revelry. Throughout the whole kingdom the choice wine flowed and the sweet music resounded. In the palace the happy pair pledged themselves in a wedding cup, while the music played and glad songs were sung. Later on, the great hall of the palace was cleared for a grand ball, and all the fishes of the sea came dressed in their best gold and silver scales, and danced till the small hours. Never had Urashima known happiness so great; never had he moved amid so much splendour.

In the morning the Princess showed Urashima over the palace, and pointed out all the wonders it contained. The whole place was fashioned out of pink and white coral, beautifully carved and inlaid everywhere with priceless pearls. But, wonderful as was the palace itself, the wide gardens that encircled it appealed to Urashima even more.

These gardens were designed so as to represent the four seasons. Turning to the east, Urashima beheld all the wealth of Spring. Butterflies flitted from flower to flower, and bees were busy among the cherry blossoms. The song of the nightingale could be heard among the trees, and the sweetest fragrance was wafted on the breeze.

Facing round to the south, he saw everything at the height of Summer. The trees were fully green, and luscious fruits weighed down their branches, while over all was the drowsy hum of the cicada.

To the west the whole landscape was ablaze with the scarlet foliage of Autumn; while, in the north, the whole outlook was beautiful with snow as far as the eye could reach.

It was a wonderful country to live in and never grow old. No wonder that Urashima forgot his home in Japan, forgot his old parents, forgot even his own name. But, after three days of indescribable happiness, he seemed to wake up to a memory of who he was and what he had been. The thought of his poor old father and mother searching everywhere for him, perhaps mourning him as dead; the surroundings of his simple home, his friends in the little village,—all these things rushed in on his mind and turned all his joy to sadness.

'Alas!' he cried, 'how can I stay here any longer? My mother will be weeping and wringing her hands, and my father bowing his old head in grief. I must go back this very day.'

So, towards evening, he sought the Princess, his bride, and said sadly:

'Alas! alas! you have been so kind to me and I have been so very, very happy, that I have forgotten and neglected my parents for three whole days. They will think I am dead and will weep for me. I must say farewell and leave you.'

Then the Princess wept and besought him to remain with her.

'Beloved!' he protested, 'in our land of Japan there is no crime so terrible as the crime of faithlessness to one's parents. I cannot face that, and you would not have me do it. Yet it will break my heart to leave you—break my heart—break my heart! I must go, beloved, but only for one day; then I will return to you.'

'Alas!' cried the Princess, 'what can we do? You must act as your heart guides you. I would give the whole world to keep you with me just one more day. But I know it cannot be. I know something of your land and your love of your parents. I will await your return: you will be gone only one day. It will be a long day for me, but, when it is over, and you have told your parents all, you will find a tortoise waiting for you by the seashore, and you will know that tortoise: it is the same that will take you back to your parents—for one day!'

'Oh, my beloved! How can I leave you? But——'

'But you must. Wait! I have something to give you before you go.'

The Princess left him hastily and soon returned with a golden casket, set with pearls and tied about with a green ribbon made from the floating seaweed.

'Take it,' said she.

'After all your other gifts?' said he, feeling rather ashamed.

'You saved my life,' said she. 'You *are* my life, and all I have is yours. That casket contains all. When you go up to the dry land you must always have this box with you, but you must never open it till you return to me. If you do—alas! alas, for you and me!'

'I promise, I promise. I will never open it till I return to you.' Urashima went on his bended knee as he said these words.

'Farewell!'

'Farewell!'

Urashima was then conducted to the gate by the court officials, led by the dolphin. There the royal sturgeon blew a loud whistle, and presently a large tortoise came up. As Urashima mounted on its back, it averted its head as if to conceal its eyes. Perhaps it had a reason. And for that same identical reason Urashima sat on its back stolidly, and never a word spoken.

Down they went into the deep, green sea, and then up into the blue. For miles and miles and miles they sped along, until they came to the coast of Japan. There Urashima stepped ashore, answered the wistful eyes of the tortoise with a long, lingering gaze of love, and hastened inland.

The tortoise plunged back into the sea, and Urashima was left on the land with a sense of sadness.

He looked about him, recognising the old landmarks. Then he went up into the village; but, as he went, he noticed with some surprise that everything seemed wonderfully changed. The hills were the same, and, in a way, the village was familiar, but the people who passed him on the road were not those he had known three days ago. Surely three short days would leave him exactly where he stood before he went. Three days could never produce this change. He was at a loss to understand it. People he did not know—strangers in the village, he supposed—passed him by as if he were a complete stranger. Some of them turned and looked at him as one would look at a newcomer. Furthermore, he noticed that the slender trees of three days since were now giant monarchs of the wayside.

At last, wondering greatly, he came to his old home. How changed it was! And, when he turned the handle of the door and walked in, crying out, 'Ho, mother! ho, father! I have come back at last!' he was met by a strange man barring the doorway.

'What do you want?'

'What do you mean? I live here. Where are my father and mother? They are expecting me.'

'I do not understand. What is your name?'

'Urashima Taro.'

'Urashima Taro!' cried the man in surprise.

'Yes, that is my name: Urashima Taro!'

The man laughed, as if he saw the joke.

'You don't mean the original Urashima Taro?' he said. 'But still, you may be some descendant of his—what?'

'I do not understand you. My name is Urashima Taro. There is no other bears that name. I am the fisherman: surely you know me.'

The man looked at Urashima very closely to see if he were joking or not.

'There *was* a Urashima Taro, a famous fisherman of three hundred years ago, but you—you are joking.'

'Nay, nay, I am not joking. It is you that are joking with your three hundred years. I left here three or four days ago, and now I have returned. Where have my father and mother gone?'

The man stared at him aghast.

'Are you mad?' he cried. '*I* have lived in this house for thirty years at least, and, as for your father and mother—why, if you are really Urashima Taro, they have been dead three hundred years; and that is absurd. Do you want me to believe you are a ghost?'

'Not so; look at my feet.' And Urashima put out one foot and then the other, in full accordance with the Japanese belief that ghosts have no feet.

'Well, well,' said the man, 'you can't be Urashima Taro, whatever you say, for he lived three hundred years ago, and you are not yet thirty.'

With this the man banged the door in Urashima's face.

What could it all mean? Urashima Taro dead. Lived three hundred years ago. What nonsense! He must be dreaming. He pinched his ear and assured himself that he was not only alive, but wide awake. And yet—and yet—everything about him seemed very much changed since he saw it last. He stood stock still on his way to the gate, and looked this way and that, trying to find something that had suffered only three days' change. But everything was unfamiliar.

Then an idea struck him. On the morning of the day that he

had rescued the tortoise from the boys, he had planted a little willow slip down by the pond in the field. He would go and look at it, and that would settle the matter.

So he took his way to the pond. Half-way he was baulked by a hedge, high and thick, which was new to him, but he found a way through a gap. Well he remembered the exact spot where he had planted the willow slip on the edge of the pond, but, when he arrived there, he could see no sign of it. In its place was a gigantic trunk bearing vast branches which towered overhead. And there the birds were singing the same songs as they sang—three days ago! Alas! could it indeed be three *centuries* ago?

Perplexed beyond measure, Urashima resolved to go to the fountain-head and settle the matter once and for all. Turning away, he made all haste to the village—was this the village he had known?—and inquired of a countryman he had never seen before, where the village chronicles were kept.

'Yonder,' said the man, pointing to a building which had certainly taken more than three days to erect.

Urashima thanked him and then hastened to the building and went in. He was not long in finding what he wanted. It was an ancient entry, and it ran:

'Urashima Taro—a famous fisherman who lived in the early part of the fourteenth century—the traditional patron demi-god of fishermen. There are many stories concerning this half-mythical character, chief of which is that he hooked a whale far from shore, and, as he would not relinquish the prize, his boat was dragged for ever and ever over the surface of the sea. Mariners of the present day solemnly aver that they have seen Urashima Taro sitting in his boat skimming the waves as he held the line by which he had caught the whale. Whatever the real history of Urashima Taro, it is certain that he lived in the village, and the legend concerning him is the subject of great interest to visitors from the great land of America.'

Urashima shut the book with a slam and went away, down to

the seashore. As he went, he realised that those three days he had spent in perfect happiness with the Princess were not three days at all, but three hundred years. His parents were long since dead, and all was changed. What else could he do but go back to the Dragon kingdom under the sea?

But when he reached the shore, he found no tortoise ready to take him back, and, after waiting a long time, he began to think his case was hopeless. Then, suddenly, he bethought himself of the little box which the Princess had given him. He drew it forth and looked at it. He had promised her not to open it, but what did it matter now? As he did not care what happened to him, the deadly secret of the box was just as well out as in. Besides, he might learn something from it, some secret way of finding his beloved Princess— and that would be happiness; but if, on the other hand, some terrible thing happened to him, what did it signify?

So he sat down on the seashore, untied the fastenings of the little box and then lifted the lid. He was surprised to find that the box was empty; but, slowly, out of the emptiness came a little thin, purple cloud which curled up and circled about his head. It was fragrant, and reminded him of the sweet perfume of the Princess's robes. Now it floated away towards the open sea and Urashima's soul seemed to go with it.

Suddenly he stood up, thinking he heard her sweet voice calling him. For a moment he stood there, a splendid figure of early youth. Then a change came over him. His eyes grew dim, his hair turned silvery white, lines came upon his face, and his form seemed to shrivel with extreme old age.

Then Urashima Taro reeled and staggered to and fro. The burden of three hundred years was too heavy for him. He threw up his arms and fell dead upon the sand.

THE FIRE BIRD

A RUSSIAN FAIRY TALE

IT was a great day when the Prince was born. The King was delighted, and the Queen nearly went mad with joy. The courtiers, though they hardly dared dance a Trepâk in the palace, could not keep their heels still; while the guards, the attendants, the little pages and pretty kitchen maids, drank tea and coffee, glass after glass, till the following morning, when they all had supper, and then crept off on tip-toe to bed. The people clapped their hands and sang and danced in the squares and streets, till those who danced the longest got sore throats, and those who sang the loudest got footsore. The whole city could not sleep for joy. The young Prince was the first-born, and would one day sit upon the throne: was this a thing to put under the pillow? On with the dance! Another song! Drink deep to the young Prince!

The doctors smiled, and stroked the smile down to the tips of their grey beards as they nodded to one another amiably. The child was strong and healthy, and would live; and besides, they all agreed upon the point that he was a Prince, and had his father's nose. But alas! doctors are not everybody. After the revel a wise man from Persia, who was staying in the city at the time, awoke from his slumbers and dressed himself, and went to see the King. Sunk in a deep sleep, he had missed the celebrations, but he had found a vision of the future; and he was now hastening to see the King about it, for, as you must understand, when a wise man knows the worst he can never keep it to himself.

When he came before the King, he had scarcely the heart to

tell him what would befall his first-born; but the King bade him speak out, and he obeyed.

'Sire,' he said humbly, 'I come not to tell thee bad news, but rather to warn thee in time, lest a vision that came to me in the night should perchance come true.'

The King looked a little anxious, for he had heard tales, strange but true, about this wise man from Persia and his wonderful powers.

'Speak on, Ferdâsan,' he said.

'Sire,' replied the seer, 'the dream that came to me was a deep-sleep vision. Doubt not that it is a warning entrusted to me to lay before you. O King, this is the substance of it. Fifteen years came and went before my inner eyes, and the son that has been born to you from heaven grew more beautiful year by year. But at the close of the fifteenth year he—flew away!'

'Flew away!' cried the King, startled. 'And what was the manner of his flight, O Ferdâsan?'

'Sire, in the midst of the palace gardens, Hausa, the Bird of the Sun, came to seek him or to be sought by him. He mounted on the back of this bird; and then, as the twilight fell, it carried him away westward.'

'With what purpose, Ferdâsan?'

'That, sire, I can reveal to you only in words that hide my thoughts, and——'

'Nay, nay; tell me all, I command you.'

'His fate stands thus. He is destined to marry the Maiden of the Dawn, and, in quest of her, he will fly westward in his fifteenth year, unless——'

'Yes, unless what, man?'

'Unless you yourself, sire, keep watch and ward and so prevent him.'

The King stared at the seer. How could he believe this thing?

'It seems that you have come to disturb my peace,' he said angrily. 'What proof have I that you speak truly? If your wisdom has brought me this warning, then your wisdom can avert the evil fate. You will remain in this palace until the die is cast. That is my command.'

'Sire,' replied Ferdâsan humbly, 'my work is done, and I must return to my cave in the mountains.'

'What!' cried the King in a rage, 'you defy me? I will compel you.'

'You cannot,' replied Ferdâsan. 'Seers stand before kings— and that is true in two ways.'

'We shall see.' The King clapped his hands fiercely. Then, as two guards came running in answer to the summons, he cried, 'Take that man and place him in a dungeon!'

The guards turned upon Ferdâsan, who stood calm and unmoved, looking at the King. Then, as they were about to seize him, a strange thing happened. They clutched at the empty air and staggered against one another, amazed. For a moment the Throne-room seemed to echo a sweet music from far away; for a moment it was filled with the faint fragrance of mountain lilies; then the King saw a thin grey mist slowly issuing through one of the windows, to dissolve in the sunlight.

And then he knew.

From that time forward, the King regarded the seer's prediction with great anxiety. He watched the young Prince continually in his first years, and, when, as was often the case, he saw him gazing wistfully towards the west when the sun had set, he felt sure that the coming event had cast its shadow before.

Accordingly, as soon as the young Prince entered his fifteenth year, the King had him imprisoned in a lofty tower situated in the palace gardens, and placed a guard about it, for he was determined to take no risk whatever.

But, while he kept the Prince a close prisoner, he surrounded him with every luxury, for he loved him dearly. He even promised him that, on his fifteenth birthday, a great festival would be held in his honour, though he himself would only be allowed to watch the festivities from the high window of the tower.

THE FIRE BIRD

The Prince implored his father to let him wander in the gardens on his birthday; but the King was so afraid that, by some means or other, he would be spirited away, that he refused. In addition to this, he double-locked and barred the topmost room of the tower in which the Prince was imprisoned.

On the day of the festival, the sun rose bright. As the Prince watched it from his high window, his heart rose with it. At noon he had fully decided to disobey his father and escape from his prison. He brooded till sunset; then, as the twilight gathered, he went to the window again and listened to the sounds of festivity in the city all around. Presently, he leaned out over the window-sill and looked down. It was a long way to the ground, but the gardens were beautiful, and he was determined to reach them and roam free among the trees and flowers. Was not this his birthday, and was not the city holding high festival in his honour? It seemed hard that he should be a prisoner, when even the guards of his prison had stolen away to join the merry throng. The city without was a blaze of light and a chorus of revel, but the gardens below seemed to be deserted: now was his opportunity.

Turning back into the apartment, he swept his eyes round for anything that would serve as a rope. There were heavy hangings falling from the high ceiling: he could not pull these down. There was the carpet; yes, he could make a rope of that.

He quickly secured a knife, and ripped from the edge of the carpet many long threads. When he had a sufficient number, he set to work to plait a rope, splicing fresh threads in at intervals until it was nearly a hundred feet long. Then he tied one end of it securely to one of the pillars supporting the roof, and let the free length of it down from the window. By the light of the full moon sailing overhead, he could see that the end of the rope reached as far as the branches of a tree growing at the foot of the tower.

It was now past midnight, and the garden below was just as silent as the city outside was loud with merriment. As the Prince climbed over the window-sill and let himself down the rope, he took

no thought as to how he might get back again; it was quite
enough to get away from the lonely, stifling place of his im-
prisonment.

At last his feet touched the topmost bough of the tree, but there
was rope to spare; and he went on until, at the end of it, he was able
to grasp a bough thick enough to bear his weight; and by this means
he climbed along to the trunk, and so to the ground.

There was no one about. The guards were all away merry-
making in the Prince's honour. Although he was still a prisoner
within the garden walls, he was enjoying his adventure and the sense
of freedom to wander, even in the gardens.

He took his way along pathways where the moonbeams strayed.
He drank in the cool night air, and paused ever and again to pluck
a sweet-smelling night-flower. Wandering on, he came at length to
a bank at the end of the garden, beyond which he knew was a steep
cliff overlooking a valley. Before his father had shut him up in the
tower, he had always been forbidden to approach that end of the
garden, and he had never done so; but now his curiosity led him on,
and he advanced cautiously along an avenue of overarching trees.
But it soon grew so dense and dark, that he was about to turn back,
when suddenly he espied a misty light beginning to grow brighter
and brighter at the far end of the avenue.

Eager to find out where this light came from, and seeing his
way more clearly now, he hastened on, and soon arrived at the mouth
of a large cave, which, inside, was as bright as day. He ventured
farther forward and peered round a buttress of rock; and there, in
the centre of the cave, a strange sight met his eyes. A gigantic bird
was standing there, getting ready to fly through the farther opening
overlooking the valley. It was stretching its neck and flapping its
wings; and, from every feather of these, flashed rays and sparkles of
light, illuminating the whole place.

In the centre of the cavern floor was a crystal pool into which,
from a ledge high up on the wall, fell a broad cascade almost like a
flowing veil, and the strong light shed by the giant bird shone through

this on to the rock behind it. And there the Prince saw the most beautiful thing he had ever set eyes on.

It was an oval picture, framed in crystal, and hanging behind the transparent cascade—a picture of a beautiful Princess. And, as he looked, her eyes met his.

Immediately the young Prince was filled with a great longing to find the original of this portrait, but it seemed that his only way of doing so was through the help of the great bird, which was now attracting his attention by strange signs. First it looked at him with a kindly eye; then it craned its neck towards the farther opening of the cave, and, flapping its wings as if about to fly, ran a step or two and then stopped and looked back at him. After doing this two or three times it crouched down and turned its head sideways, looking straight at him, as much as to say, 'Don't you want to ride in the air?'

The Prince saw the bird's meaning, but, to signify that he wanted to find the Princess, he pointed to the picture. At this the bird spread its wings right out until the tips brushed against each side of the cave, the feathers quivering intensely and throwing out a bright light which almost blinded the Prince.

Then the bird drew in its wings and made a sign to him to mount between them. At this the Prince, feeling sure that the giant bird meant to take him to the Princess, climbed up and seated himself between the great wings.

In another moment the bird had launched itself from the farther opening of the cave, and they were soon sailing high over the valley. Some revellers in the city looked up and saw what they took to be a meteor flashing across the sky; but it was really the Fire Bird bearing the Prince swiftly to the far-off palace of the Princess.

How many thousands of miles they flew between the darkest hour and dawn, the Prince could not tell. Nestling warm and comfortable among the soft feathers, he heard the roar of the great creature's wings, and knew they were travelling at a tremendous pace. And at last the Fire Bird craned its neck downwards, and, as they began to descend in a slanting direction, the Prince could see something sparkling on the horizon in the first rosy light of dawn.

Nearer and nearer they came, and now he could distinguish the great gates and towers of what seemed to be a palace of pure crystal, surrounded by beautiful gardens.

Swiftly they swooped downwards, and the Fire Bird alighted on the edge of a broad balcony, and crouched down for the Prince to dismount.

The journey had not been in vain. There, on a mossy bank among the beautiful flowers in the garden, he found the Princess asleep; and, as he looked down at her, he saw that her face was the face he had seen in the portrait.

He tried to wake her, but her sleep was sound : she did not stir. He breathed on her eyelids and whispered in her ear, but still she slept on.

Seeing this, the Bird grew restless, and craning its neck forward, seized the Prince with its beak and placed him again between its wings. Then it sprang upwards and soared swiftly into the sky.

Soon they were back in the cave, and the Prince, dreading to return to the prison tower, spent the hours of daylight in his warm nest between the Fire Bird's wings.

The following night, as the hours were drawing on towards dawn, the Bird set forth again. But again the Prince was unable to wake the sleeping Princess, so they returned once more. But, on the third night, when they reached the Princess, the light of dawn was in the sky, and, as it grew every moment rosier and rosier, the Princess awoke of her own accord to find the young Prince sitting among the flowers by her side. She had only just time to see the Fire Bird pluck a feather from its wing with its beak, and let it fall at her feet, before it soared away. She picked up the feather and placed it in her bosom. Then she looked at the Prince.

There is love, and there is love; but such love as sprang up at the same moment in two hearts can never be described. It was as if she had been dreaming about him all her life, and now she had awakened to find him. It was as if his journey had been to Paradise. She raised her arms to him, and he enfolded her and kissed her. Then they wandered among the flowers and trees, and all the birds understood: they sang so divinely.

Towards evening, as the shadows began to fall, the Princess's sister, who was a wicked Sorceress, came into the garden and stood behind a tree watching the lovers.

'I'll soon put an end to this,' she said, clenching her hands in jealous rage. She went away and performed spells, and, by her wicked arts, she summoned the image of the Prince before her, so that his life went out of his body, and he remained in the Princess's arms like one dead.

Terrified and distracted with grief, the Princess carried the lifeless body of her lover into the palace and laid it on a couch in her own apartment. There, exhausted with the effort, she fell upon it, weeping bitterly. She called his name, but he did not answer. His ears were deaf, his eyes were closed, his pale lips did not respond to her kisses.

But the Prince was not dead: he was bewitched. The Sorceress, by means of his image, had torn his heart from his breast and had taken it far away. Yet, all the time, that heart was still beating with life, and with love for the Princess.

Forlorn and sorrowful the Princess sat by the couch, when suddenly she started up with clenched hands.

'I know! I know!' she cried. Then she bent down and kissed the Prince's lips. She felt them tremble against hers, and, though she could not call him back, she knew that he was not dead. 'Oh! my wicked sister! This is your work. You have bewitched my love! Never again! This is the end!'

She ran everywhere, in and about the palace, in search of her sister, her hands clenched, her eyes blazing, her teeth set. But she could not find her. At last a page, terrified to death at her aspect, confessed that her sister had fled from the palace alone, mounted on the fleetest steed of the stables.

The Princess at once resolved to follow her and force her to restore the Prince to life and health. But, at the very outset, there was a terrible difficulty to be surmounted. The Princess herself had never been beyond the walls that encircled the vast grounds of the palace. She knew that there were twelve gates, and that only one of these was left unlocked from sunset till sunrise, and that none could tell which one it might be. Now the law of the palace permitted her to try one gate each night, and one gate only.

She sat down and thought, and then decided to try the same gate each night until it happened to be the right one. For twelve nights she tried, but each time she found the gate locked and barred.

Then she suddenly remembered that, when the Fire Bird had brought the Prince to her, it had plucked a bright feather from its wing and let it fall at her feet. She had preserved it in a golden casket. Could it be that this feather had magic powers? She ran with all haste to her apartment, and took it from the casket. As she did so, it sparkled and quivered. As she held it up she was more than ever convinced that it held magic powers.

She looked at the feather, and she thought of the Fire Bird itself, and wished that it could only come and advise her what to do.

Scarcely had she conceived the wish, when a faint sound from far away struck upon her ears. As she listened, it grew louder and louder, and nearer and nearer, until at last she knew it was the roar of the Fire Bird's wings. She ran out onto the balcony, and there she saw it, like a meteor in the sky, every moment growing bigger.

At last, with a glad, shrill cry, it swooped down, and its giant wings fluttered and vibrated a moment before it alighted on the edge of the balcony, its fiery golden light sparkling on the crystal pillars and shimmering in the air all around.

The Princess held up the feather, and the Fire Bird bowed its head slowly three times. Then it suddenly turned round as if to fly away, but looked back at her, and raised its wings, and fluffed out the soft, glistening feathers in the hollow of its back. Arching its head round, it began to act as if it were preparing a nest for her between its wings, and the Princess saw plainly that it was only waiting for her to seat herself there before flying away. The Bird knew what she wanted; she was sure of that. So she mounted between the wings, and nestled down on a soft feather bed of dazzling golden light, warm and comfortable. Then, with a long, jubilant cry the Bird rose in the air, and, craning its neck westward, flashed through space at a terrific rate.

Very soon they overtook the setting sun, passed it, and left it sinking on the horizon as they went on into the purlieus of the Land of Night and Silence, which lies beyond the great round shoulder of the world. And here the Fire Bird blazed along, leaving a trail of light in its wake and throwing a radiance on the hills and forests over which it passed; until it came, by way of the Valley-which-has-no-Borders, to the Forest-without-an-End.

Here the Bird swooped downwards and alighted before a black-mouthed cave. He crouched while the Princess dismounted. As she did so, the Bird plucked two fresh feathers from its wing with its beak and held them out to her. They shed a brilliant light, and she, seeing at once that they would serve as lamps, took them, one in each hand, and advanced into the gloomy cave.

She had not gone far when she heard a voice crooning a witch song, and, peering round the edge of a rock, she espied her sister seated beside a cauldron, beneath which was a freezing fire fed with blocks of frozen brine.

From the witch song her sister was singing, the Princess learned that her lover's heart was in the cauldron. She listened while the Sorceress sang:

'Seethe! Seethe! Heart of her lover,
Beating in tune with mine.
Never the two their love can recover,
Never their arms entwine.
Freeze! Freeze! Heart in this cauldron,
Seared by the frozen brine!'

With a scream the Princess rushed forward, and, before her

wicked sister could prevent her, she had upset the cauldron with a crash. Some of the icy fire of brine splashed up in the face of the Sorceress, and with a loud, grating shriek, she fell to the ground senseless—dead!

The Princess snatched up her lover's heart, and placed it in her bosom against her own, where she could feel it still beating. Then, without waiting another moment, she ran back to the Fire Bird, and sprang upon its back with a cry of joy, patting its neck and stroking its feathers.

Up in the sky they soared again, and away over the world towards the palace in the Home of the Dawn. And, as they neared their destination, the Princess suddenly missed something. Quickly she felt in her bosom to see if the heart of her lover was safe; but lo, it was gone! It seemed to have grown warm and melted right away.

Distressed at this, she urged the Fire Bird to still greater speed, until his track through the sky was like that of a shooting star. At length they swooped down and alighted on the balcony of the palace. The roaring of the Fire Bird's wings was stilled, but the hum of its feathers continued—a throbbing pulsation of musical sound.

As the Princess alighted, the Prince himself came running to her. Then, with a mingled cry of delight, the lovers leapt to greet each other, and, when they were enfolded in each other's arms, the Fire Bird discreetly turned his head away and preened his tail feathers.

The Princess did not trouble about her lover's heart which she had taken from the Sorceress and missed on the way. She now felt it beating against her own, and knew that it was in its right place. The Prince was free from the wicked spell at last.

The Fire Bird's work was done. Without a word he sprang into the air, and was soon lost to sight. And the lovers did not hear him go, for, by some mysterious power, he hushed his wings and went secretly, for, as you must have seen, he was really a very old bird.

The Prince and the Princess were married very soon, and, during the celebrations, the Fire Bird was seen to circle thrice every night round the palace, but he never settled.

As King and Queen of the People of the Dawn, they reigned for long years, and the Fire Bird was always their friend. On every anniversary of their wedding day, they awoke to the sound of his roaring wings. He always brought a present; and do you know what it was? Just a single feather of his shining wing, so that they might obtain whatever joy they wished for.

THE STORY OF THE BIRD FENG

A CHINESE FAIRY TALE

In the Book of the Ten Thousand Wonders there are three hundred and thirty-three stories about the bird called *Feng*, and this is one of them.

Ta-Khai, Prince of Tartary, dreamt one night that he saw in a place where he had never been before an enchantingly beautiful young maiden who could only be a princess. He fell desperately in love with her, but before he could either move or speak, she had vanished. When he awoke he called for his ink and brushes, and, in the most accomplished willow-leaf style, he drew her image on a piece of precious silk, and in one corner he wrote these lines:

> The flowers of the pæony
> > Will they ever bloom?
> A day without her
> > Is like a hundred years

He then summoned his ministers, and, showing them the portrait, asked if any one could tell him the name of the beautiful maiden; but they all shook their heads and stroked their beards. They knew not who she was.

So displeased was the prince that he sent them away in disgrace to the most remote provinces of his kingdom. All the courtiers, the generals, the officers, and every man and woman, high and low, who lived in the palace came in turn to look at the picture. But they all had to confess their ignorance. Ta-Khai then called upon the

171

magicians of the kingdom to find out by their art the name of the princess of his dreams, but their answers were so widely different that the prince, suspecting their ability, condemned them all to have their noses cut off. The portrait was shown in the outer court of the palace from sunrise till sunset, and exalted travellers came in every day, gazed upon the beautiful face, and came out again. None could tell who she was.

Meanwhile the days were weighing heavily upon the shoulders of Ta-Khai, and his sufferings cannot be described; he ate no more, he drank no more, and ended by forgetting which was day and which was night, what was in and what was out, what was left and what was right. He spent his time roaming over the mountains and through the woods crying aloud to the gods to end his life and his sorrow.

It was thus, one day, that he came to the edge of a precipice. The valley below was strewn with rocks, and the thought came to his mind that he had been led to this place to put a term to his misery. He was about to throw himself into the depths below when suddenly the bird *Feng* flew across the valley and appeared before him, saying:

'Why is Ta-Khai, the mighty Prince of Tartary, standing in this place of desolation with a shadow on his brow?'

Ta-Khai replied: 'The pine tree finds its nourishment where it stands, the tiger can run after the deer in the forests, the eagle can fly over the mountains and the plains, but how can I find the one for whom my heart is thirsting?'

And he told the bird his story.

The *Feng*, which in reality was a *Feng-Hwang*, that is, a female *Feng*, rejoined:

'Without the help of Supreme Heaven it is not easy to acquire wisdom, but it is a sign of the benevolence of the spiritual beings that I should have come between you and destruction. I can make myself large enough to carry the largest town upon my back, or small enough to pass through the smallest keyhole, and I know all the princesses in all the palaces of the earth. I have taught them the six intonations of my voice, and I am their friend. Therefore show me the picture, O Ta-Khai, and I will tell you the name of her whom you saw in your dream.'

They went to the palace, and, when the portrait was shown, the bird became as large as an elephant, and exclaimed, 'Sit on my back, O Ta-Khai, and I will carry you to the place of your dream. There you will find her of the transparent face with the drooping eyelids under the crown of dark hair such as you have depicted, for these are the features of Sai-Jen, the daughter of the King of China, and alone can be likened to the full moon rising under a black cloud.'

At nightfall they were flying over the palace of the king just above a magnificent garden. And in the garden sat Sai-Jen, singing and playing upon the lute. The *Feng-Hwang* deposited the prince outside the wall near a place where bamboos were growing and showed him how to cut twelve bamboos between the knots to make the flute which is called Pai-Siao and has a sound sweeter than the evening breeze on the forest stream.

And as he blew gently across the pipes, they echoed the sound of the princess's voice so harmoniously that she cried:

'I hear the distant notes of the song that comes from my own lips, and I can see nothing but the flowers and the trees; it is the melody the heart alone can sing that has suffered sorrow on sorrow, and to which alone the heart can listen that is full of longing.'

At that moment the wonderful bird, like a fire of many colours come down from heaven, alighted before the princess, dropping at her feet the portrait. She opened her eyes in utter astonishment at the sight of her own image. And when she had read the lines inscribed in the corner, she asked, trembling:

'Tell me, O *Feng-Hwang*, who is he, so near, but whom I cannot see, that knows the sound of my voice and has never heard me, and can remember my face and has never seen me?'

THE STORY OF THE BIRD FENG

Then the bird spoke and told her the story of Ta-Khai's dream, adding :

'I come from him with this message ; I brought him here on my wings. For many days he has longed for this hour, let him now behold the image of his dream and heal the wound in his heart.'

Swift and overpowering is the rush of the waves on the pebbles of the shore, and like a little pebble felt Sai-Jen when Ta-Khai stood before her. . . .

The *Feng-Hwang* illuminated the garden sumptuously, and a breath of love was stirring the flowers under the stars.

It was in the palace of the King of China that were celebrated in the most ancient and magnificent style the nuptials of Sai-Jen and Ta-Khai, Prince of Tartary.

And this is one of the three hundred and thirty-three stories about the bird *Feng* as it is told in the Book of the Ten Thousand Wonders.